CW01499586

Other Books by Harriet Steel

Becoming Lola

Salvation

City of Dreams

Following the Dream

Dancing and Other Stories

The Inspector de Silva Mysteries

Trouble in Nuala

Dark Clouds over Nuala

Offstage in Nuala

Fatal Finds in Nuala

Christmas in Nuala

Passage from Nuala

Rough Time in Nuala

Taken in Nuala

High Wire in Nuala

Cold Case in Nuala

Break from Nuala

Stardust in Nuala

Long Odds in Nuala

Retreat from Nuala

AN INSPECTOR DE SILVA MYSTERY

CHANGING TIMES IN NUALA

HARRIET STEEL

Author's Note and Acknowledgments

Welcome to the fifteenth book in the Inspector de Silva mystery series. Like the previous ones, this is a self-contained story, but wearing my reader's hat I usually find that my enjoyment of a series is increased by reading the books in order and getting to know major characters well. With that in mind, I have included thumbnail sketches of those taking part in this story who have featured regularly in the series.

Several years ago, I had the great good fortune to visit the island of Sri Lanka, the former Ceylon. I fell in love with the country straight away, awed by its tremendous natural beauty and the charm and friendliness of its people. I had been planning to write a detective series for some time, and when I came home I decided to set it in Ceylon in the 1930s, a time when British Colonial rule created interesting contrasts, and sometimes conflicts, with traditional culture. Thus Inspector Shanti de Silva and his friends were born.

I owe a debt of gratitude to everyone who helped with this book. John Hudspith was as usual an invaluable editor. Julia Gibbs did a marvellous job of proofreading the manuscript, and Jane Dixon Smith designed another excellent cover and layout for me. My thanks also go to all those readers who have told me they enjoyed the previous books in the series and would like to know what Inspector de Silva and his friends did next. Their enthusiasm has encouraged me to keep writing. Above all, my heartfelt gratitude goes to my husband Roger for his unfailing encouragement and support, to say nothing of his patience when Inspector de Silva's world distracts me from this one.

Apart from well-known historical figures, all characters in this book are fictitious. Nuala is also fictitious, although loosely based on the hill town of Nuwara Eliya. Any mistakes are my own.

Characters featuring in this book who appear regularly in the Inspector de Silva Mysteries:

Inspector Shanti de Silva. He began his police career in Ceylon's capital city, Colombo, but in middle age he married and accepted a promotion to inspector in charge of the small force in the hill town of Nuala. He likes a quiet life with his beloved wife and their cats, Billy and Bella. He enjoys his food and is a keen gardener.

Jane de Silva. She came to Ceylon as a governess to a wealthy colonial family and met and married Shanti de Silva a few years later. A no-nonsense lady with a dry sense of humour, she is very fond of detective novels and enjoys discussing his cases with her husband.

Sergeant Prasanna. In his thirties and married with a son and daughter. He is doing well in his job and taking increasing responsibility. He likes cricket and is exceptionally good at it.

Constable Nadar. A little younger than Prasanna. Diffident at first, he has gained in confidence over the years. He is married with two boys and likes making toys for them.

Archie Clutterbuck. The British assistant government agent in Nuala and as such responsible for administration and keeping law and order in the area. He is fond of fishing, golf, and the company of his Labrador, Lady.

Florence Clutterbuck. Archie's wife, a stout, forthright lady. She likes to be queen bee and organise other people.

Doctor David Hebden. Doctor for the Nuala area. Under his professional shell, he is rather shy. He likes cricket and dislikes formality.

Emerald Hebden (née Watson). She arrived in Nuala with a touring British theatre company, decided to stay and subsequently married David Hebden with whom she has a daughter named Olivia. Emerald is popular in local society and a good friend to Jane. Her full story is told in *Offstage in Nuala*.

Sanjeewa Gunesekera. The manager of the best hotel in Nuala, the Crown, and an old friend of Shanti de Silva.

CHAPTER 1

Autumn 1947
A Sunday morning

Happy with his inspection of his vegetable plot, Inspector Shanti de Silva moved on to the greenhouse. In a shady corner of the garden, it was pleasantly cool inside. Wooden shelves lined the wall at the rear, and he looked along them, considering his neatly stacked terracotta pots. He chose four and moved them to the wooden staging opposite where a small heap of compost lay ready. Bella, who had followed him into the greenhouse, sprang up onto the staging and settled down to watch as he found a trowel and used it to scoop compost into each flowerpot before tamping it down with his fingers, smelling its rich, nutty aroma as he worked.

Next, he reached for a large pot containing a scented geranium. As his hand brushed the soft leaves, the tangy zest of lemons wafted into the air. He liked to grow the old-fashioned geraniums. They had been prized by Victorian gardeners for their great variety of scents, from citrus like this one, to rose, peppermint, sandalwood, and even nutmeg. Their flowers didn't possess the showy razzmatazz of the varieties that had become more popular in his own day, but they did have a delicate charm.

He picked up a pair of clippers, snipped off a few

cuttings and potted them up. As he returned the geranium to its place, he noticed a silver trail winding up another of his pots of stock plants. At the top, a snail was about to inch its way over the lip and into the compost. Gently, he prised it off, took it outside and put it down in a patch of cabbages that were past using in the kitchen. 'You can eat your fill of those,' he said, 'but not of my geraniums.'

Back in the greenhouse, he watered the cuttings then stood back to admire his handiwork. Once they started to grow, he would tell Anif their gardener to plant them out, but one plant would be brought into the house. Jane loved the way the scent filled a room.

'Lunch is ready, sahib.'

De Silva looked up to see their servant Delisha in the doorway. Bella jumped down from the bench and rubbed up against her, asking to be stroked. 'Shall I tell the mem-sahib that you are coming?' asked Delisha as she obliged.

'Yes, please.' He cleaned his hands on a rag hanging from a hook then followed her and Bella out.

'I'd better go and wash,' he said when he found Jane in the drawing room.

'Don't be long or the food will get cold.'

'I won't be.'

In the bathroom, as he soaped and rinsed his hands, he decided he had done enough gardening for the day. After lunch he would relax on the verandah and read the Sunday papers. He wondered what the news would be from Ceylon's giant neighbour. After being partitioned into two nations, India for the Hindus, and Pakistan for the Muslims, they had achieved independence from the British a few months previously. Partition had been seen as the best solution to the strife between the two religious communities, but it had sparked off one of the largest migrations that the world had ever seen. Hundreds of thousands of people had been forced to leave their homes, often in fear of their lives. The very thought of how they must have suffered filled de Silva with dismay. Huge numbers had perished. The violence and disruption had still not come to an end and showed little sign of doing so in a hurry. Soon, Ceylon would be independent too, although it would have the status of a Dominion of the British Empire and still owe allegiance to the British monarch. Thankfully, there seemed to be a good chance of the handover being conducted in a peaceful manner. He prayed that would continue to be the case, but it was undeniable that change often brought problems in its wake.

He dried his hands and went to join Jane in the dining room. 'How was church?' he asked as they ate.

'Oh, much the same as usual, except that Reverend Peters' sermon was more interesting this week than last. David and Emerald Hebden were there and sent their good wishes, as did Archie and Florence.'

De Silva ate some of his fish curry and rice and wondered what his boss, Archie, and Archie's wife Florence thought about the prospect of independence. He knew his and Jane's friends the Hebdens intended to stay on. Ceylon would still need doctors. But what would the future hold for Archie and Florence? No doubt there would be a period of transition, but after that, there would be no role for a couple who had been part of the British ruling class. He wondered if Archie would miss being in a position of power and authority.

'He might adjust to it a little more easily than Florence,' said Jane when he voiced the thought. 'After all, it's likely to mean that he has more time for golf and fishing.'

'Very true.' He broke off a piece of naan bread and wiped up the remains of the curry sauce on his plate. 'That was delicious.'

'Would you like some more?'

De Silva thought of his waistline then grinned. 'It's

Sunday, why not. And maybe a bit more of the lime pickle to go with it.'

Lunch over, he went out to the verandah, leaving Jane to discuss the menu for the week with cook. The front page of the Sunday paper confirmed that the news was as gloomy as ever. He read a couple of articles then thought about tackling the crossword. Learning to unravel the torturous ingenuity of the *Nuala Times'* crossword setter was part of his preparation for the retirement that he saw looming on the horizon. To his great satisfaction, he managed to work out two clues before he decided to wait for Jane to help him. To pass the time, he turned to the nature notes column, one that he always found soothing.

'Anything interesting in the paper?' asked Jane when she joined him.

'Still bad news from India and Pakistan.'

Jane sighed. 'One wonders when it will end. It's all so sad. Independence should be a happy beginning.'

'I fear that the human race has a talent for making things complicated, often producing the opposite result to the desired one. There is some more cheerful news though.'

'That's good, what is it?'

'The writer of the nature notes column describes a night hike he took in a valley near Hatton where there's an abandoned tea plantation. Apparently, it's hard to get to but the effort is worthwhile. He found many interesting species of insects there.'

Jane made a face. 'I'm not sure I'd go wandering around at night in remote places just to find creepy-crawlies.'

De Silva chuckled. 'I expect many people would say the same, but there were moths too. In particular, many giant Atlas moths, clouds of them he says. I see one or two occasionally in the garden but nothing like that.'

'I suppose they might just make the journey worthwhile,' Jane said with a smile. 'But I'm happy to let you go if you like and come back to tell me about it. I've reached a stage in life when I prefer to spend my nights comfortably in bed.'

'To be honest, I think I have too. I'm satisfied with reading his description.'

'That's probably just as well.' Jane sat down and he held the paper out to her. 'Would you like to do the crossword? I've started but I haven't got far.'

'In a minute, first I'd like to look at the society pages. Emerald mentioned at church that there were photographs of the wedding of an old friend of hers to William MacDonald.'

'The tea planter?'

'Yes. Emerald was great friends with the bride, Venetia, when they were growing up, but they lost touch after that. She didn't even know Venetia was in Ceylon until she came to Nuala last year. She'd got the job of secretary to the chairman of the tennis club. As you know, Emerald's very keen on tennis so she's often up there, and she and Venetia recognised each other straight away.'

Jane found the page, and although de Silva wasn't terribly interested in weddings, especially when he didn't personally know either of the parties, he glanced at the pictures. The new Mrs MacDonald was extremely pretty with softly waved blonde hair, a retroussé nose, and a lovely smile. She also looked considerably younger than William who was, de Silva guessed, well into his forties.

Jane shook her head reprovingly when he remarked on the disparity between the couple's ages. 'Emerald says they're very much in love. I hope you're not suggesting she's just after his money.'

De Silva grinned. 'I apologise to the absent Mrs MacDonald, but can I help it if that crossed my mind? He's reputed to be very wealthy, and it's hard to break the habit of a lifetime in the police force. I was taught to question everything and leave no stone unturned.'

Jane sighed. 'I know, but I hope you're wrong in this case. Emerald says that William's charming, and they seem so happy together.' She studied the photo of the couple posed in front of an arbour smothered with roses, and surrounded by wedding guests. 'He's a very good-looking man.'

'Hmm, then I'm glad we don't move in the same social circles. I wouldn't want your head being turned.'

'As if it would be.'

'I'm relieved to hear it.' De Silva looked at the photograph. 'There's someone here who doesn't look as if she's enjoying the day.' He pointed to a lady in a high-necked dress that looked to be made out of some kind of stiff fabric. Her hair was arranged in an equally rigid style.

'That's Elspeth MacDonald, William's sister. We're on a few of the same committees and we've been introduced, but I've hardly spoken to her apart from that. I hear she's a difficult lady to get to know.'

She turned the page, found the crossword, and picked up the pencil that lay on the table by her chair. 'Well, now that I've satisfied my curiosity, let's get on with the crossword. Oh, by the way, I forgot to tell you that the entry form for the flower show has arrived. Once we've finished the crossword, you could spend some time deciding which classes you'd like to enter.'

As Jane considered the next clue, de Silva's mind drifted back to his earlier thoughts of retirement. Might it mean that which classes to enter in Nuala's flower shows would soon be the most important kind of decision he had to make?

He glanced at Billy and Bella who were sprawled out, toasting themselves in a nearby patch of sunshine. They seemed to have happily perfected the art of spending a large part of their day relaxing, but from his own point of view, he found it hard to make up his mind whether a lot of time to relax would be a good thing or not.

CHAPTER 2

The day of the flower show arrived, and the well-tended grass of the Residence's main lawn was dotted with stalls and tables displaying fruit, vegetables, and flowers. Apples and pears were exhibited alongside more exotic species such as figs, peaches, and pomegranates. There were jewel-like raspberries and strawberries, neatly laid out on small plates and decorated with a few of their own leaves. Immaculate vegetables looked glossy in the sunshine, and flowers filled the air with perfume. Every bloom had been chosen for its perfection. They were displayed in small bunches or even singly, but Nuala's flower-arranging ladies also demonstrated their skills with splendid exhibits. Adding to the charm of the occasion, most of the British ladies wore bright flower-printed frocks. Buttonholes added a splash of colour to the cream linen jackets of the men.

As was customary, the judges had made their rounds before the show was officially declared open, with Florence Clutterbuck then doing the honours by cutting the ribbon at an improvised archway to the lawn. De Silva was gratified to see that his dahlias, his favourite scarlet Bishop of Llandaff variety, had been awarded a silver medal. His chillies and onions had each received a bronze, and his leeks a highly commended but, he reflected, a lot of the credit ought to go to Anif. He must be sure to give him something extra when the next payday came around.

The flower show didn't only highlight the skills of Nuala's gardeners. The arts of baking and preserving were not neglected. There were classes for cakes, jams, chutneys, and relishes. The pots of preserves had small saucers beside them that contained the judges' tasting teaspoons, and sweet, fruity smells mingled with the aroma of spices in the humid air.

'A real slice of old England, eh,' said a familiar voice behind de Silva. He turned to find Archie smiling jovially at him, his face pink and damp under his Panama hat. 'Talking of slices,' he went on, 'that Victoria sponge looks good.' He indicated an appetising-looking cake with a filling of strawberry jam and a liberal dusting of icing sugar on top. 'Florence insisted on my buying dozens of raffle tickets so perhaps I'll be in luck. The ladies usually donate their efforts as prizes.'

De Silva wondered if, in many cases, the efforts were those of the ladies' cooks. Jane sometimes worked alongside their own cook and showed him how to make British cakes and preserves, but she might be an exception to the rule.

'Fine day for it,' Archie went on. 'There's many an English village that would give a lot to have weather like this for their jollities. My recollection of flower shows at home is that they usually ended in rain, even if they didn't begin that way.' His gaze moved from de Silva's face to a point somewhere beyond his right shoulder. 'Ah, the MacDonalds are here.'

De Silva turned and saw the wealthy tea planter William MacDonald and his wife. William was tall with dark hair and features that would have looked patrician if he hadn't been laughing and chatting animatedly with the group of people he was with. He wore the customary pale linen suit and Panama hat favoured by the British, but they looked to be of particularly fine quality. His navy-blue and white striped shirt was complemented by a navy-blue handkerchief in the breast pocket of his jacket, and he wore a scarlet carnation in his buttonhole. His wife Venetia stood beside him with her arm tucked in his. Her frock, patterned with blush-pink roses, flattered her slim figure. In the flesh, she was even prettier than she had looked in their wedding photograph in the *Nuala Times*.

'She's certainly a stunner, Venetia MacDonald,' Archie went on. 'Very charming too.' With amusement, de Silva noticed his boss's sentimental tone. He remembered an occasion years ago when an old flame of Archie's had come to Nuala, giving rise to a glimpse of a romantic streak beneath the gruff exterior.

'Quite a turn-up for the book,' Archie was saying. 'Everyone thought Bill MacDonald was a confirmed bachelor, although I understand quite a few ladies have set their caps at him over the years. I expect you know that he owns Waverley, that big plantation a few miles outside town.'

'I know of it, of course, and I've often passed by, although I've never had occasion to visit it.'

'The house is an ugly great place to my mind, all turrets, and battlements in the style the Victorians favoured when they wanted to emulate a medieval castle. It's not at all in keeping with its surroundings, still, each to their own. Bill's grandfather came out to Ceylon from Scotland in the 1840s. Apparently, he was a great admirer of Sir Walter Scott's Waverley novels and named it after them. Anyway, by all accounts the grandfather had a shrewd head for business. When he died, he left his son Angus, Bill's father, a tidy fortune. Angus seems to have been a different kettle of fish to his father. Never took much interest in the business, but luckily for the family it appears to have prospered despite that.'

'Did he have other interests?'

'I believe he was very keen on butterflies and moths. Wrote a lot of learned papers about the species to be found in these parts. He was still alive when I first came to Nuala, but I can't say I got to know him. I don't think anybody did. He seemed happy to shut himself away in his ancestral pile, and his wife appears to have felt much the same. Never joined in with any of the ladies' activities. It's a wonder that Bill is as full of the spirit of camaraderie as he is. He's a popular fellow and good company. We often play golf together. I expect being sent away to school was the saving of him.'

From what de Silva had heard of British boarding schools, he imagined that William MacDonald had been forced to sink or swim. Luckily for him, he seemed to have swum.

The MacDonalds finished the conversation with their friends and strolled away. As they did so, de Silva noticed that the lady who had looked so sour in the wedding photograph was following them. He couldn't remember her name.

'That's Bill's sister Elspeth,' said Archie. 'She's a few years older than him. She's lived at Waverley all her life and never married. I wouldn't be at all surprised if Bill's tying the knot hasn't put her nose badly out of joint. After their mother died, Angus never remarried, and according to my wife, Elspeth has been used to ruling the roost at Waverley.'

De Silva watched Elspeth stomp after her brother and sister-in-law, her green and blue tartan skirt, severe cream blouse and thick stockings contrasting unfavourably with Venetia's fresh and attractive outfit. He felt rather sorry for her. It must be difficult to cope with a radical change in one's life. However charming Venetia was it would be hard for a sister-in-law in Elspeth's position not to resent her.

Archie looked at his watch. 'I'd better be off to the tea tent and find my wife. It never does to keep a lady waiting.'

Especially if that lady was Florence, thought de Silva. Aloud he said, 'And I ought to find Jane. I expect she's busy with friends, but we may see you in the tent.'

'Excellent.' Archie gestured to the display of dahlias where the silver medal card was propped up against the vase containing de Silva's entry. 'By the way, congratulations. Jolly good show.'

'Thank you.'

As Archie walked away, de Silva put up a hand to shade his eyes from the sun and scanned the crowds for a sign of Jane. He couldn't see her, so he decided to set off in the direction of the tea tent and hope to find her on the way. He was turning for a last glance at his prize-winning dahlias when he noticed the middle-aged lady who stood a few feet away from him. Tall, and wearing a dark blue dress that emphasised an angular figure, she was packing some dahlias and the vase that had contained them into a wicker basket. A gold medal card still lay on the table. She caught him looking at her and gave him a diffident smile.

'Allow me to congratulate you, ma'am,' he said, smiling back.

'And congratulations to you too, Inspector. I saw your name on your silver medal card.'

'Ah, and may I ask yours?'

'Of course, I'm Helena Bradshaw. Bishop of Llandaff is such a lovely variety. I wish I'd had some to exhibit this year but unfortunately the slugs got to them before they had a chance to flower.'

'Slugs *are* a problem.'

'Yes, and they seem particularly fond of this moist, warm climate. I hate to kill them, so I usually ask our gardener to look for them after dark and take them to the wild patch at the far end of our garden. But this year …' She broke off and to de Silva's surprise, looked almost tearful before she continued. 'This year I had other things on my mind.'

'There is always a great deal to think about in the garden,' he said soothingly. 'You can console yourself that you gave a good meal to some very happy slugs.'

'I suppose that's the best way look at it.'

'Helena! There you are!' a male voice boomed out and the lady visibly tensed. She lifted a hand to brush an invisible strand of hair from her cheek. 'I'm nearly ready, dear. I was just packing up my dahlias.'

The short, irascible-looking man who had spoken joined them. He spared de Silva the barest of glances and a peremptory nod before turning back to the lady. 'The car's waiting and I'm in a hurry to get home.' He reached for the gold medal card and threw it on top of the flowers in the wicker basket. 'There, that's done. Now let's be off. I've spent quite enough time for one day looking at poxy flowers and flattering old trouts like Florence Clutterbuck.'

Helena winced. 'Cyril, please …'

The man gave a bark of laughter 'You know I never mince my words.' He snatched up the basket and marched off across the grass. Her cheeks flushed, Helena bade de Silva goodbye and followed; de Silva watched as they disappeared into the crowd.

'Ah, good, I've found you at last, Shanti.' Jane joined him. 'I saw you talking to Helena Bradshaw and her husband.'

'How do you know them?'

'Oh, they come to church, but I don't know them well. If we meet, we only pass the time of day. I believe they live on the Hatton side of town, and Helena doesn't belong to any of the groups that I do.'

'In the case of the husband, I'm not sure I'd describe our brief exchange as a conversation, but she seems a charming lady, although rather anxious.'

'Hardly surprising when she's married to a man like Cyril.' Jane lowered her voice. 'I've heard from various people who play at the bridge club that he's not at all popular there. Apparently, he can be quite rude if someone makes a mistake, which isn't hard to do as bridge is such a complicated game. He's especially unkind to Helena which is horrid for her and embarrassing for everyone else. They feel very sorry for her.'

'I must say I'm glad you've never asked me to learn bridge. Compared to what I've heard about it, police work seems restful.'

'But seriously, how they play games often tells you a lot about people.' A troubled expression came over Jane's face. 'There are even rumours that he ill-treats Helena in other ways, but there's no evidence of that, and of course if someone doesn't ask for help, it's not the done thing to interfere.'

That was very sad but true, thought de Silva. He wondered how many wives felt obliged to keep painful and humiliating secrets hidden from the world.

'Perhaps if there's a suitable opportunity to get to know her better, I ought to take it,' mused Jane. 'She might be glad of someone to talk to.'

'That's a kind thought. Now, if you'd like a cup of tea, shall we go to the tea tent?'

* * *

The air in the tea tent was stuffy and resounding with conversation, laughter, and the hiss of tea urns. De Silva wondered if it would be possible to find an Elephant ginger beer, rather than a cup of tea. A nearby table was unoccupied, so he sat Jane down at it and went to join the queue at the refreshment counter. Whilst he waited, he noticed Archie and Florence talking to William and Venetia Mac-Donald. With them were several of the other colonial officials he had come across in his years in Nuala, but one man was a stranger to him. He would, however, have been hard to miss in any crowd. He looked to be about the same age as William MacDonald and was also tall, but whereas

MacDonald's hair was neatly barbered, this man's was unruly and grew down over his ears. Much more colourfully attired than the usual run of British men, he wore canary yellow trousers and a red jacket. He wasn't wearing a tie, and his green shirt was unstarched. Instead of the laced-up leather shoes that British men mostly wore, his slip-on shoes were made of a soft, light brown suede.

'What will you have to drink, Inspector sahib?'

De Silva turned away from this symphony of colour to find one of the Residence servants, who often opened the door to him on his visits to Archie, smiling at him.

'Good afternoon, Yatish. Do you have any Elephant ginger beer?'

'Of course, sahib.'

'Then a glass of that for me and a cup of tea for my wife, please.'

'Coming up, sahib. Will you have something to eat? We have English biscuits and butter cake.'

De Silva rubbed his hands. 'I think we could manage both, thank you.'

The tea and ginger beer poured and placed on a tray with a plate containing some biscuits and two generous slices of cake, de Silva handed over a few coins. Carrying the tray carefully to avoid knocking into anyone in the crowd, he returned to Jane.

'Gracious! A feast! You'll make me fat.'

'Nonsense, I'm afraid I'm the one at risk of that, but the flower show only happens once a year.'

Jane took a sip of tea. 'Mm, perfect, that's just what I needed. Thank you, dear.'

'My pleasure.' He drank some of his ginger beer and the tangy liquid cooled his throat. 'Much as I like tea, I find an Elephant ginger beer perfectly hits the spot on a hot afternoon.'

Jane put down her teacup and took a Rich Tea biscuit

from the selection on the plate. 'Do you think a flower show will be held next year?'

De Silva thought for a moment.

'I can't see why not,' he said. 'Of course, this changeover is going to be a big thing, but as long as we don't have troubles like India's and Pakistan's, I think there's a good chance that many aspects of ordinary life won't be very different, at least for quite some time. After all, Archie and Florence will be staying on in Nuala for the moment so that Archie can help the new administration in the first few months of independence. He and Florence will probably have to move out of the Residence into somewhat more modest accommodation, but if I know Florence, she'll manage to persuade the new people in charge that the local community will still appreciate having the traditional events. Flower shows, race meetings, and cricket matches bring people together, and then there's the motor rally. Nuala's famous for it. I'm sure no one would want to bring it to an end.'

'Do you know yet who will be in charge of the police force?'

'I hope to find that out very soon. After all, I'll have to answer to him, whoever he is, instead of Archie from February onwards.'

Jane sighed. 'When you name the month, it sounds so close.'

'It is.' He picked up a slice of cake and took a bite. 'I hope there will still be butter cake,' he said through a mouthful of crumbs.

Jane gave him a little punch on the arm. 'Of course there will, you silly thing.'

'Good, then I think I can face a changed world.'

'Hello, you two.' David and Emerald Hebden stopped beside the de Silvas' table. 'May we join you?' asked Emerald.

De Silva jumped to his feet. 'Of course, please take my seat. I'll find extra chairs.'

Hebden fetched tea for himself and Emerald, and they were soon settled around the table chatting. After a few minutes, de Silva's thoughts drifted back to Jane's question. It was one that led to many more issues than flower shows, cricket matches, horse racing, and the celebrated Nuala car rally. Ceylon had been a colony for more than five hundred years, first occupied by the Portuguese, then the Dutch and finally the British. There was no getting away from the fact that the country was facing the end of an era, with everything that entailed. Despite what he'd said to Jane, de Silva sometimes woke in the night filled with anxiety; creating a successful and fair future for an independent Ceylon was bound to be a massive task.

'You're very quiet, Shanti.' Emerald's voice broke in on his thoughts.

He pushed them quickly away. 'Forgive me,' he said with a smile. 'At my age one gets a little sleepy in the afternoon.'

'Hot in here too,' said Hebden. 'I could do with a breath of air. If you ladies have finished your tea, shall we take a stroll?'

'That's a good idea,' said Jane. Emerald nodded.

Outside, shadows were beginning to lengthen, and the crowds had already thinned out. Servants busied themselves dismantling the show's tables and stalls. The Residence, its white walls tinged with gold by the low sun, queened it over the scene like a stately dowager.

De Silva and Hebden walked a little way behind Jane and Emerald. 'Well, a very successful day,' Hebden said. 'You kept up your record on prizes, and our gardener didn't do too badly either. I can't claim any of the credit as I leave the garden to him. Still, today had the flavour of the end of an era, would you agree?'

'Yes, I've been thinking the same.'

'Where will we all be in a year's time, I wonder.'

'Let's hope here in Nuala, peaceful and content.'

'I agree. Emerald and I have no wish to leave, and as for our little Olivia, she loves it here. Nuala's a wonderful place for a child to grow up, and she would hate to be parted from her beloved pets.'

'What does she have now?'

'Two tortoises, a mynah bird, and a kitten. She tried to persuade me to let her have a baby elephant, but I refused, on the grounds that baby elephants eventually grow up.'

De Silva chuckled.

'Still,' Hebden went on, 'there's no denying much will change.' He gave de Silva a sideways glance. 'Will you be glad to be rid of British rule?'

'I hope you won't take it the wrong way if I say yes, but I do have some misgivings. Any change brings its challenges, and this will be a huge one.'

'The price of running one's own show, eh?'

'Exactly.'

Emerald and Jane had slowed their pace to let them catch up.

'Your conversation sounds very serious,' said Emerald. 'It's far too lovely an evening for politics.'

Hebden took her arm. 'I'm sorry, my love. What shall we all talk about instead?'

'Jane and I were talking about the artist.'

'What artist would that be?'

'Oh, you know, the one who came to paint Archie's portrait. I'm sure I told you about it. Someone in the Colonial Office thought it would be a good idea to commission portraits of senior outgoing British officials. Of course, Florence was thrilled that Archie was included. If she's mentioned it once, she's mentioned it a dozen times. She was thinking of having a grand unveiling today, but unfortunately the portrait isn't quite finished.'

'Ah, I remember now that you did say something about it, but I'd forgotten. Anyway, I'd never heard of him.'

'And you're such an expert on art, my love.'

Hebden laughed. 'No, but I know how to mend a broken bone. You'll have to remind me of his name, although I shall probably forget it again.'

'Tranter,' said Emerald. 'Laurence Tranter. He was here today. You might have noticed him. He was hard to miss in his yellow trousers and red jacket.'

'Ah yes, I saw him. He was talking to your friends the MacDonalds.'

'That would be right. Venetia told me the other day that he'll be staying on in Nuala for a while. William is very keen for him to paint her portrait.'

'A charming idea. Would you like him to paint yours afterwards?'

'Certainly not. I couldn't bear all that sitting still. Anyway, I suspect he may be rather expensive.' She pulled her shawl around her shoulders. 'It's getting a little chilly. Shall we be off home soon? I promised Olivia I'd be back in time to read her a bedtime story.'

'Give her our love,' said Jane. 'I'm sorry she wasn't well enough to come today.'

'It's nothing serious,' said Hebden. 'Just one of those childhood ailments. She'll be right as rain tomorrow I expect and back to getting up to mischief.'

'Isn't that what children are supposed to do?'

They parted company and de Silva and Jane went to collect his dahlias and vegetables. Once everything was packed away, they returned to the Morris and drove home.

Billy and Bella were waiting for them in the hall. 'They must have heard the car,' said Jane.

De Silva bent down to pick up Bella, who nuzzled her small, warm head into the hollow of his neck, purring like a little dynamo. Billy, always the more independent of the two, waited a moment whilst Jane reached down to stroke him, then trotted away in the direction of the kitchen.

'It's time for their evening meal,' said Jane as she unpinned her hat. 'But I shan't be hungry after all that tea and cake.' She laughed. 'No need to look so crestfallen, Shanti. I'm not suggesting we miss dinner. Amongst other things, cook has made your favourite pea and cashew curry.'

De Silva rubbed his hands together. 'Excellent. I'll go and wash, then I think it will be time for a drink on the verandah. Shall we listen to some music after dinner?'

'That would be nice. That new recording of Chopin preludes would be lovely and relaxing after a busy day.'

'Then Chopin it is.'

CHAPTER 3

January 1948

De Silva sat in his office working his way through the pile of paperwork on his desk. With Nuala's preparations for the celebrations to mark Independence Day on the fourth of February approaching, the weeks since the flower show had been busy ones. There was to be a grand parade through town ending up at the Residence, where the new flag of Ceylon, displaying the golden lion of Kandy, the symbol of the kings of old, would be hauled up the flagpole.

It would be a proud moment, but de Silva had lost many an hour of sleep trying to think of everything he ought to do to ensure that the day ran smoothly. The whole town would be out on the streets, everyone eager to celebrate, and large crowds were notoriously unpredictable, especially when plenty of arrack would no doubt be consumed. If it became necessary to take action to keep the crowds in order, his, Prasanna's, and Nadar's combined efforts would be akin to sending a mouse to catch a cat. The solution had been to swear in some of the Residence's more senior servants as special constables for the occasion, but they had needed training in what their duties would be. That had taken up some of his time, although Prasanna and Nadar had shouldered a considerable amount of the work, and he had been proud of the way they had performed their task.

Policing the crowds wasn't the only thing he had needed to think about. There had been many meetings with Archie to decide on the precise route the procession should take. With hundreds of dancers, musicians, and even elephants taking part, it was important to avoid places where there might be a bottleneck, causing the participants to collide in a jumble. The fire brigade needed to be involved too. There would be a firework display at the Residence after dark which would, de Silva was confident, be well organised, but he was sure that the locals would want to set off their own firecrackers and that would be far less predictable. He needed to be sure that Nuala's water trucks could be brought up to as many places as possible if accidental fires needed to be put out.

A yawn escaped him; he had not slept well. It had rained heavily in the middle of the night, as if a gigantic cloud had poised itself over Nuala with the express purpose of deluging the town. The rain had beaten down some of his flowers and he had left instructions for Anif to deadhead those that seemed unlikely to recover.

There was a knock at the door. He stopped reading and called out to enter. Nadar appeared in the doorway bearing a cup of tea.

'I thought you might be glad of this, sir.'

'I certainly would.' De Silva made a space amongst his paperwork. 'Put it down there.'

He leaned back in his chair and rolled his shoulders to ease them. 'I suppose your sons are excited about the big day.'

Nadar grinned. 'They've talked of little else for the past few weeks, sir. They're looking forward to going with their friends to enjoy the fun. It seems no time since they were babies,' he added a little sadly.

'Yes, time passes quickly, and you'll find that the older you get, the faster it goes by. Now, have you typed up that report for Mr Clutterbuck that I gave you yesterday?'

'Yes, sir.'

'Good, I'll give it a quick look over then you can send it to the Residence.'

Nadar left the room, closing the door behind him, and de Silva sat for a few moments as he drank his tea, contemplating the future. He might not have many more years left to him to see where independence took Ceylon, but Prasanna and Nadar and their families would, he hoped, live long and happy lives under the new regime.

He had just finished his tea when the telephone on his desk rang. He picked up the receiver and once more heard Nadar's voice. 'Doctor Hebden would like to speak to you, sir. He's calling from the hospital at Hatton. Shall I put him through?'

'By all means.'

From the tone of his friend's voice, de Silva quickly realised that it wasn't a social call. Hebden explained that his patient, William MacDonald, had been taken dangerously ill the previous day. 'It was late afternoon,' Hebden said, 'and he'd not long returned home. The rest of the family was out, so it was their head servant, a fellow by the name of Pamu, who called me. He sounded so alarmed by his master's condition that rather than wasting time going to see for myself, I immediately called for the ambulance to take him to hospital before I drove to the house. The ambulance arrived at the same time I did, and by then his wife Venetia and his sister Elspeth had returned home. Venetia was extremely distressed. In fact so much so that I thought it best to administer a mild sedative. Elspeth was much more composed, but of course very concerned that everything possible should be done for her brother.'

'Naturally, and I'm very sorry to hear all this. I believe the MacDonalds haven't been married long.'

'Yes, only a few months. How did you know that?'

'I remember Jane pointing out their wedding photograph

in the *Nuala Times*. She was interested because Emerald had told her that she and Venetia are old friends.'

'That's right, Emerald's very upset about what's happened.'

De Silva reached for his notepad and a pencil. 'Archie also told me a bit about the couple at the flower show. Now, I assume you have a particular reason for telling me all this.'

'Yes, I'm afraid I do. The violence and abruptness of William's condition normally indicates a heart attack, and that's the view that Bradley-Clarke, the consultant in charge here at the hospital, is taking. William's receiving the customary treatment of rest, sedation, and oxygen. At first, that seemed to me to be the logical explanation, but now that I've had time to reflect, I'm not convinced Bradley-Clarke is on the right track.'

'Why do you say that?'

'Even though he's been my patient for a good many years, William rarely troubles me for advice. The last time he came to see me was shortly before he and Venetia tied the knot. He told me he was concerned by the disparity in their ages and intended to take out substantial life insurance. The company he was looking at required a medical report. I conducted various tests and was able to provide one confirming that he was in excellent health with a strong heart and a robust constitution.'

'I see.' De Silva jotted down a few notes. 'So what do you think has happened?'

'He may have ingested poison of some kind. I considered the possibility of a snakebite, but there are no puncture marks on his body.'

'Are you suggesting that someone poisoned him?'

'I'm not sure. It could be accidental. Of course, all this is only my theory. Bradley-Clarke's patently unimpressed by the opinion of a mere GP, although for the sake of thoroughness, he's ordered samples of blood and urine to be sent off to the laboratory for testing. Tests are, however, not always infallible and may reveal nothing.'

'Who else knows about this?'

'William's sister, Elspeth, who independently of my view is absolutely convinced her brother was poisoned. By all means tell Jane. I know we can rely on her discretion. Naturally, I trust Emerald too, although unless the tests back up my theory, I'm undecided as to whether to mention anything to her. As far as the rest of the world, including the Waverley servants, is concerned, however, it's probably best to give out Bradley-Clarke's version of what's happened. One doesn't want to provoke scurrilous rumours.'

'I agree. So, what does this consultant have to say about his patient's chances?'

'He's confident that the worst of the danger is over.'

'Is it possible to talk to William yet?'

'No, he's still heavily sedated. Bradley-Clarke intends to continue with that course of action for the moment. Agreeing to the tests was the only concession he was prepared to make, and it's not in my power to argue with him. I'm sorry, I know that's not a great deal of help to you. If William was poisoned, or accidentally ingested something poisonous, one would like to know who he was with and what he ate and drank in the hours leading up to his collapse.'

De Silva's pencil hovered over his notepad. If it became absolutely necessary, Archie might be persuaded to overrule the consultant, but he knew that such men were looked on as gods in their own kingdoms. In any case, before commencing battle he had to consider the possibility that Hebden was wrong. 'Let's hope the strong constitution you mentioned helps him to recover very soon,' he said.

'Amen to that, but I'm afraid there's more. Venetia and Elspeth came down to the hospital with me. In view of her extreme anxiety, I thought it best for me to drive Venetia, but Elspeth drove herself. By the time the immediate crisis had passed, it was almost midnight. In other circumstances, I might have asked the hospital if they would provide beds for the night, but there'd been an accident earlier in the day. A bus collided with a bullock cart just outside Hatton. Thankfully, no one was killed, but many passengers were injured and brought to the hospital for treatment. Elspeth said that in any case she thought it would be best to spend what was left of the night in their own beds. She insisted she was in a fit state to drive home, so I didn't put up any objection and she left with Venetia. Douglas followed them in his car.'

'Douglas?'

'Ah sorry, I forgot to mention him. He's the other MacDonald sibling, a bit younger than William. He wasn't at home when we left Waverley, but when he returned later, Pamu told him what had happened, and he drove straight to the hospital.'

'Are they still there now?'

'That's the thing. This morning, Elspeth and Douglas returned to the hospital on their own. I'd driven back myself to see how William was progressing, and I met them coming in. They told me that Venetia had disappeared.'

De Silva frowned. 'What?'

'Elspeth's claiming it's because she's the one who poisoned William and now that there's a good chance he'll pull through, she's afraid she'll be found out. When they arrived back at Waverley last night, Venetia apparently said she was exhausted and wanted to go straight to bed. Douglas retired too, but Elspeth stayed up for a short while to give some instructions to the servants before going to bed herself. This morning, Venetia was gone. Her bed didn't look to have been slept in.'

'Was anything missing? Clothes for example?'

'Elspeth says only what Venetia had been wearing that day.'

'Any sign of a struggle?'

'No.'

De Silva jotted down a few more notes. 'So, what's your theory?'

'I must admit, I'm at a loss. Venetia can drive, but apparently all the family's cars were present and correct. Waverley is fairly remote. I can't see that she would have set off for anywhere on foot.'

'What do you think of Elspeth's allegation?'

'Even if it's true that William was poisoned, I find it hard to believe Venetia was responsible, but I've only instinct to back that up. If she's innocent, she might have been in an agitated state and gone out to get some air then suffered a mishap of some kind.'

'Did the brother have anything to say? It seems from what you've told me that his sister does all the talking.'

'That's about the size of it. Unfortunately for him, Douglas doesn't have his brother's abilities or his sister's strong character. He's tried various occupations but always ended up coming back to Waverley when they go wrong. In theory, he helps his brother to run the plantation, but in practice he spends a lot of his time lunching or playing cricket. He's a pretty handy player, I'll give him that.'

That was high praise from Hebden, who was himself an excellent cricketer, thought de Silva.

'Elspeth intends to stay with William,' Hebden went on, 'but Douglas returned to Waverley to join the servants in searching the grounds. So far, there's been no message that they've found Venetia.'

'Hmm, I'd better get over there and see what I can do.'

'Thank you.' There was a note of relief in Hebden's voice. 'Do you know how to get there?'

'Yes, I've passed the turning many times.'

'Good.'

They ended the call, and de Silva stood up from his desk,

buttoned his jacket, and took his cap from the hat stand. In the public room, Prasanna and Nadar looked up from their work.

'Is everything alright, sir?' asked Nadar. 'Doctor Hebden sounded very concerned.'

'I'm afraid he may have reason to be.' He explained about William MacDonald's sudden collapse, Venetia's disappearance, and Elspeth's accusation. 'I've agreed to go over to the house to see what progress is being made with the search for the lady. Prasanna, you'd better come with me. You hold the fort here, Nadar.'

* * *

Archie was right about Waverley being ugly, thought de Silva as he reached the end of the long drive. The house was built of grey stone with a roofline bristling with turrets, crenellations, and chimneys. Two massive circular towers flanked the façade. The windows were framed in a darker stone with stone mullions and transoms and in some places, there were arrow slits. The overall impression was of a romantic idea of a medieval castle.

He parked the Morris, and with Prasanna following, walked up to an imposing four-square entrance porch topped by a frieze decorated with heraldic griffons and snarling lions. The front door looked distinctly unwelcoming with a brass doorknocker in the shape of a grotesque, scowling face. 'Right,' he said, hoping his tone was more confident than he felt, 'we'd better get on with this.' He pressed the bell push to one side of the door and heard a sepulchral sound inside the house. A moment or two later, the door opened with a creak. The servant who stood there looked somewhat alarmed at the sight of them. De Silva wondered if he thought they were bringing more bad news.

Quickly, he explained that they had come to help with the search and asked to see whoever was in charge of it.

'It is Pamu, sahib,' said the servant. 'I will take you to him.'

That was interesting, thought de Silva, he didn't mention Douglas.

The servant stepped aside for them to enter, and they found themselves in a cavernous hall with a stone-flagged floor. The lower half of the walls were covered with dark linen-fold panelling and the upper half painted blood red. A lofty ceiling was decorated with more dark wood, carved in elaborate traceries. In the centre was a large skylight made of stained glass. A stone bench ran around the walls, punctuated at intervals by pedestals that supported gleaming suits of medieval armour. De Silva looked at the swords and lances displayed with these incorporeal knights and felt a shiver of discomfort. Of all the violent deaths a man could suffer, death on a medieval battlefield must have been amongst the grimmest. He wondered how anyone had even been able to fight, encased in such a weight of metal and with their view impeded by a lowered visor.

'This way, if you please, sahib,' said the servant.

As he and Prasanna followed the man down a wide corridor lined with tapestries, de Silva brought his mind back to the matter in hand. At the far end, the servant stood aside and ushered them into a large drawing room. De Silva heard Prasanna give a little gasp. The austere grandeur of the hall had been impressive, but this room was beautiful. Below a gilded dado rail, the walls were painted deep sage green. More gilding glittered on the ribs that sprang from the rail and followed the curve of the ceiling to meet at the point where a magnificent crystal chandelier was suspended. Between the ribs, the walls were decorated with wallpaper that had an intricate design of leaves, flowers, and fruit. The servant went to the gilded double doors that led to the garden and opened them. Outside was a terrace bounded by a stone balustrade, and at its centre, a broad flight of steps leading down to a lawn.

The servant pointed to the lake on the far side of it where a group of men were hauling a heavy object from the water. 'I think they have found something, sahib.'

De Silva felt a pang of sadness. Was this yet more tragedy for the MacDonald family? 'We'd better get down there and see what it is.'

At the lake, a man who looked older than the rest greeted him. 'Good morning, Inspector. Doctor Hebden telephoned to say you would be coming.'

'Are you Pamu?'

'Yes.' Pamu pointed to the carcass on the ground. It was half decomposed and entangled in slimy green weed, but still recognisable as that of a small deer. 'We have been dragging the lake all morning. The memsahib instructed us to do so before she left for Hatton, but this is the first thing we've found.'

'Poor creature, it looks to have been in there for quite a long time.'

Pamu nodded.

'How many men do you have for your search?'

'Thirty, Inspector. Twenty are servants who work in the house and grounds, then there are ten from the plantation. Others who are still there are also searching the buildings and fields. The sahib's brother is with them.'

Ah, that explained his absence, thought de Silva.

'Is there any more news of Sahib William?' asked Pamu.

'What did Doctor Hebden tell you?'

'That he is recovering slowly, but still in hospital. The doctors say he suffered a heart attack.'

'Sorry, I don't know anything more than that.'

Pamu looked anxious. 'But it is good news that he's recovering, isn't it?'

'Yes, of course. I think we can be confident your master will soon be as right as rain. Have you worked for the family for long?'

'For twenty years, Inspector.'

And is Sahib William a popular boss?'

'Yes, we will all be very happy when he returns.'

De Silva shaded his eyes against the sun and glanced across the lake to the broad sweep of parkland beyond it. It was just as well that Pamu had plenty of men at his disposal. He turned back to him. 'You seem to have everything under control, so I'll leave you and go down to Hatton to find out what's going on there. My sergeant will stay with you to help.'

'Thank you, sahib.'

'I'd be obliged if someone could drive him back to town later. I may be gone for some time.'

'Of course, sahib.'

'Thank you. Prasanna, a word before I go.'

They stepped away, leaving Pamu to direct operations for the removal of the deer carcass.

'They look to be doing a good job,' said de Silva when they were out of earshot. 'Provided Venetia MacDonald hasn't strayed off the plantation, there should be a fair chance of finding her. But whether she'll be dead or alive is anyone's guess,' he added grimly. 'There's a telephone here. If you have any news, call me at the hospital, or if you can't get me there, ring Nadar and leave a message with him. Say nothing to Pamu or any of the servants, but keep in mind Doctor Hebden's suspicion that William MacDonald was poisoned. Your searches here may throw up something relevant.'

'Do you think there's a connection to Mrs MacDonald's disappearance, sir?'

'At this stage, I wouldn't like to say.'

Prasanna nodded.

'And when you think you've done all you can to help here, ask Pamu to organise your lift back to town.'

'Yes, sir.'

CHAPTER 4

Hatton hospital was a two-storey, whitewashed building set around three sides of a courtyard. Its red-tiled roof jutted over a wide balcony with an iron balustrade where patients close to recovery were brought to sit and enjoy the sunshine and a change of scene. On the ground floor was a loggia with the hospital entrance in the centre. De Silva went in and asked if Doctor Hebden was still there. The receptionist nodded. 'I'll send someone to fetch him.'

He thanked her and went to sit on one of the chairs ranged along the wall opposite the desk. It was pleasantly cool in the reception hall and the pale green walls – a colour he thought of as British government building green – was soothing. When Hebden arrived a few minutes later, he stood up to greet him. 'How's your patient?'

'Still sedated, but his colour is better than it was. It's a blessing that they're as well equipped here as they are, so we didn't need to get him to Colombo. His brother has gone back to Waverley, but Elspeth is still here and insisting she won't leave William's side. Do you have any news of Venetia?'

'I'm afraid not. I've also been up to Waverley and spoken with Pamu. He seems to be doing an excellent job, but so far all he and his men have found is the carcass of a deer in the lake. I didn't see Douglas, who had already arrived but was searching elsewhere.'

'Elspeth told me she was up at dawn and sent her maid to call Venetia straight away because she wanted to get back to the hospital as soon as possible. We don't know exactly what time Venetia left the house, but it must have been before then, so she's been missing—' he glanced at the clock above the reception desk '—for at least eight hours.' Hebden frowned. 'I don't like the sound of it.'

De Silva had to agree with him. In cases of missing persons, the chances of finding them unharmed usually dwindled in proportion to the amount of time that elapsed before they were found. Unless Venetia was deliberately avoiding detection, the outlook wasn't good.

'Is there any news about the tests?'

'Not yet. When the samples were sent to the laboratory at Kandy, I asked for the urgency of the matter to be stressed, but as I said before, they may reveal nothing, so it would still be impossible to know what antidote to administer. It's lucky that whatever struck William down, it looks like he will recover. Of course, if we are dealing with poison, the human body is capable of excreting some poisons perfectly well on its own.'

What a tragedy, thought de Silva, that if, or as it now seemed when, William MacDonald pulled through, it might be to find that his beloved wife had met with a fatal accident, or worse, plotted to kill him.

'Shall we go up to the room?' asked Hebden. 'I expect Elspeth will want to hear the news from Waverley first hand.'

De Silva followed him through a pair of swing doors then down a short corridor to a staircase lit by a window high up in the wall. Their footsteps echoed as they climbed the stairs, arriving at a long corridor painted the same shade of green as the reception hall. Hebden led the way, stopping at the fourth door down on the right. 'This is it,' he said. 'I should warn you that Elspeth isn't an easy lady to deal with at the best of times, and her concern for her brother hasn't done anything to improve her temper.'

'Thank you for the warning.'

Hebden opened the door and went into the room. It had two windows but as the blinds were lowered, the light was dim, and it took de Silva's eyes a moment to adjust. When they did, he saw William MacDonald's tall, thin form stretched out on the metal-framed hospital bed under a light blanket. An oxygen mask covered his nose and mouth. There was a powerful smell of antiseptic in the air.

The lady who was sitting on the upright chair beside the bed turned to face the door. De Silva recognised her from the flower show.

'Ah, Doctor Hebden, you're back.' She spoke quietly, then with a brusque gesture indicated they should go into the corridor. As Hebden closed the door to the room behind them, she gave de Silva a sharp glance. 'And who are you?'

'Inspector Shanti de Silva, ma'am. Chief of Police in Nuala.'

'I see. Have you found my sister-in-law?'

'Not yet, ma'am. However, I've left my sergeant at Waverley to help with the search. I've just come from there, and I was impressed by the efforts being made to locate Mrs MacDonald. I think it's too soon to give up hope.'

Elspeth gave him a dry smile. 'Oh, that's what you think is it, Inspector? In other circumstances I might agree with you, but not this time. My brother William hasn't had a day's illness in his life. Whatever the hospital say about a heart attack, I'm sure that Venetia tried to poison him and doesn't want to be found. She made a beeline for him from the very first moment she saw him. She was determined to snare him, and she did. I always suspected that she was only after his money, and now I'm convinced of it. As soon as she knew that he'd changed his will to leave her the bulk of his estate, as well as taking out that life insurance that you helped him with,' she threw Hebden a chilly glance, 'she put her mind to how she was going to get rid of him. She was all ready to play the part of the grieving widow, but now William will survive, and that role has been snatched away, she's panicked. She's seized on the only course left to her that might save her skin before her crime is unmasked. She's run away.'

'Waverley is fairly remote, ma'am, and I understand that all of the family's cars were accounted for. If, as you say, your sister-in-law ran away, how would she manage to get far?'

Elspeth scowled. 'She has an accomplice of course. Recently, I've suspected that she's been seeing someone in secret. On several occasions, I've surprised her talking in private on the telephone. She puts down the receiver pretty sharply when she realises that I'm within earshot and makes some weak excuse about arranging an appointment or talking to a friend, but she doesn't fool me.'

'Can you recall any particular times when these calls have occurred?'

Elspeth's face darkened. 'I have too much to do to take notes on everything that happens at Waverley, Inspector. I hope you're not suggesting that I imagined them?'

'Of course not, ma'am.'

Suddenly, Elspeth's expression changed, and de Silva saw her wipe away a tear. There was a catch in her voice. 'If only I'd managed to persuade poor William not to marry Venetia. But he wouldn't listen. She was probably cheating on him from the beginning,' she added bitterly.

Hebden put a hand on her shoulder. 'Try not to distress yourself, ma'am. Your brother's condition is steadily improving. There's good reason to think that he'll be back to his usual robust self in a few days.'

As swiftly as she had given way to her feelings, Elspeth rallied. 'Thank you,' she said bluntly. 'Well, what do you have to say now, Inspector?'

'The accusation you've made is very serious, ma'am,' said de Silva as gently as he could.

'So you still doubt my word, do you? Perhaps the police force here in Hatton will take a different view.' Her eyes narrowed, but de Silva kept his composure.

'I was about to say that it will of course be thoroughly investigated. At this stage, nothing can be ruled out. Every possibility must be assessed against whatever evidence we uncover.'

Elspeth's chin jutted out, giving her the air of an angry bulldog. 'Then I suggest you get on with finding my sister-in-law and asking her what she was doing yesterday before my brother collapsed.'

'I have every intention of doing so, ma'am. I assume there are photographs of her at Waverley. I hope you have no objection to my taking one of them so that I can have copies circulated to help in the search for her.'

'As you wish, Inspector. Now, if you'll excuse me, I'd like to get back to my brother's bedside.'

* * *

'Phew!' Hebden pulled a handkerchief out of his pocket and mopped his brow. 'I'm sorry about that, de Silva.'

'There's no need for you to apologise. You did warn me.'

'So, what do you make of Elspeth's accusation now?'

'It would be wrong to dismiss it. It's an old maxim in police work that one should look close to home for a culprit and find out who stands to benefit from a crime.'

'Do you mean that if William has left the bulk of his estate to Venetia as Elspeth said, the finger points to her?'

'Yes, but it's possible that Elspeth's accusation is motivated by jealousy. At the flower show last November, Archie Clutterbuck pointed her out to me and said he wouldn't be surprised if her brother's marriage to Venetia hadn't put her nose out of joint. It's understandable that she would be bitter if she's been used to being in charge in the MacDonald household. Quite apart from taking up William's affection and attention, Venetia may want to make changes that Elspeth dislikes.'

Hebden nodded. 'I gather from what Venetia's told Emerald that she finds Elspeth very unfriendly. Venetia has tried hard to win her over, but without success.'

'Now that I've met the lady, I can't say I'm surprised.'

'What do you propose to do?'

'Since it's not possible to speak to William at the moment, I'll have to pursue other avenues. You told me it was Pamu who called you out. Did he say how soon it was after William arrived home that he collapsed? Had he mentioned where he'd been beforehand?'

'I'm afraid that in the heat of the moment, I never asked. I was more concerned with getting him to hospital as quickly as possible. Of course, when we got there one of the questions Bradley-Clarke asked was whether William had been complaining of any pains earlier that day. Unfortunately, neither Venetia nor Elspeth could help much as they hadn't been with him since breakfast. After that he left for his office on the plantation. Venetia drove to Hatton to do some shopping, but she didn't say which shops she went to. I'm afraid I didn't press her for more details.' Hebden looked a little sheepish. 'Initially, I didn't think it might be important.'

'A perfectly reasonable conclusion.'

'But of course once the thought of poison entered my mind, the question of where and how William spent the day became significant.'

'What about Elspeth?'

'She said she spent the morning at the vicarage at a meeting of one of her church committees and stayed to lunch. But surely you don't suspect her of poisoning William?'

'She seems an unlikely culprit, I agree, but all the same I ought to verify her story. In fact Jane may be able to help. She's also on several of the church committees and might have been present. I'll see to that. I ought to speak to Douglas MacDonald too and I assume William has a secretary. One of them may be able to give me details of what William was doing earlier in the day. I'll go back to Waverley this afternoon and try to speak to them. I'll also have another word with Pamu.' He looked at his watch. 'I've not had lunch yet. Will you join me for a bite to eat?'

Hebden shook his head. 'I'd like to say yes, but I'd better not. Yesterday I'd planned to pay a visit to a fellow medic who has a practice on the Hatton side of town. We often collaborate in the ordering of drugs and equipment, so we meet from time to time to share ideas and discuss our needs. This time the visit had to be postponed because my secretary had a call from his to say that one of his patients had died suddenly. He needed to visit the family and would be busy for the rest of the day with the necessary arrangements. To cut a long story short, he's expecting me to look in today between his afternoon and evening surgeries.'

'Very well.'

'I wonder, is there any chance you could telephone Jane and ask if she would visit Emerald? I may not be home for several hours. After I've seen my colleague, I have a few appointments of my own to keep. Emerald knows Venetia's missing because when I found out about it, I rang her from the hospital to ask if she knew where her friend was. She'll be anxious to hear what's been going on since then and I'm sure she'd be grateful for some company.'

'I'm sure Jane would be happy to help. What about this accusation of Elspeth's?'

Hebden sighed. 'I suppose I ought not to delay telling

Emerald for much longer, but I'd rather not tell her over the telephone, and I may not be home until late.' He hesitated. 'It's a bit of an imposition, I know, but might Jane be prepared to do it if it seems advisable?'

'I'll talk to her.'

'Thank you.'

As they walked across the car park, Hebden pointed out the green MG parked near to his Austin and the Morris. 'That belongs to Elspeth. She's a talented driver. Won quite a few cups I believe, including the first ladies' trophy to be awarded at the Nuala rally.'

'No mean feat.' De Silva unlocked the Morris's door. 'Will you let me know when you hear about the test results?'

'Of course.' Hebden rubbed a hand over his chin. 'Whether or not the lab comes up with anything positive, it occurs to me that it might be worth talking with an acquaintance of mine. He used to be a director of the Botanic Gardens at Peradeniya. He's made a bit of a speciality of poisonous plants over his career. Of course, he may not be able to throw any light on the problem so you might think it a waste of time.'

'Not at all. My watchword is always to leave no stone unturned. In this case,' he added, 'I also see I'll have my work cut out proving to Elspeth MacDonald that my approach is suitably thorough.'

Hebden chuckled. 'I'm afraid she was rather uncomplimentary. But perhaps one should give more leeway than one normally would. If nothing else, she seems to be genuinely fond of her brother, and as far as Emerald's heard, he's very fond of her, despite her rough edges.' Hebden climbed into his Austin and put the key in the ignition. 'Good luck with your inquiries, and let's speak soon.'

'I'm sure we will.'

* * *

De Silva drove into the centre of Hatton and found a place to park near the bazaar. As this wasn't his home turf where the Morris was known to belong to the Chief of Police, he summoned a couple of boys who were looking admiringly at the car and gave them a few coins to keep an eye on her with the promise of more when he came back.

He set off into the crowded alleyways between the stalls. Hatton's bazaar, considerably larger than Nuala's, attracted many more shoppers and most of the stalls sold a greater abundance of goods. The vegetable stalls that he passed displayed huge baskets of onions, aubergines, jackfruit, potatoes, and peas in their pods. Spicy aromas wafted from leafy bundles of coriander and fenugreek, and strings of chillies sparkled like shiny scarlet and green necklaces.

The fruit stalls were also well stocked with pineapples, melons, mangoes, rambutans, wood apples, coconuts, and the sweet-sour-tasting red starfruit. Stalls selling meat were fewer and further between, mainly furnished with plucked fowl dangling by their scrawny legs. De Silva always thought there was something sorrowful about their dead eyes and limp, goose-bumped bodies. He rarely ate meat, and in the past few years, Jane too had got out of the habit. He sometimes asked her if she had done so purely to please him and was secretly hankering after the roast lunches that seemed to be the high point of British cuisine, but she insisted she was not.

He left the area of fruit and vegetable sellers and continued past the stalls that sold trinkets, clothes, and household items to reach the area where the food sellers set up their outdoor kitchens. Delightful aromas and the sizzle of food cooking on red-hot metal made his mouth water. He stopped at one of his favourite stalls and ordered a bowl of kottu roti. The stallholder chopped red onion, chillis, yellow peppers and a handful of curry leaves, and cooked them up with strips of paratha, finishing with a ladleful of vegetable curry from a nearby simmering pot. De Silva handed over payment in exchange for the bowl then looked around for a place to sit.

He was on his way to a bench in the shade when he noticed a man, a European, watching him; he looked vaguely familiar but at first de Silva couldn't place him. His camp stool was set up on a patch of earth too close to the roots of a coconut palm for anyone to put a stall there. In front of him was a small portable easel and by his side a leather box with the lid open to show an assortment of brushes, rags, small bottles, and tubes of paint.

The smell of turpentine wafted towards de Silva. He noticed a half-finished painting on the easel. It was of the bazaar, but not rendered in a realistic fashion; instead, there were elongated figures and brightly coloured objects distorted as if they were being seen through a prism. It was very different from the paintings de Silva had seen at the Residence or in the British homes he had visited over the years, but it seemed to him to express the world of the bazaar so vividly that he decided he liked it very much.

The artist smiled and gestured with his brush to de Silva's lunch. 'That looks good. I think I'll get some myself.'

'Try the third stall down that alleyway.' De Silva pointed to the entrance. 'They make one of the best kottu roti in Hatton.'

'Thanks for the tip.' The artist picked up a cloth and carefully wiped the brush he had been using then placed a larger piece of cloth over his work. 'Keeps the flies off,' he said. 'Right, time for lunch. Keep an eye on my stuff for me, will you?'

'Certainly.'

The artist chuckled. 'Not every day it gets police protection.'

By the time he came back from the stall with his food, de Silva was halfway through his own meal. He made space on the bench and the artist sat down beside him.

'I'm no expert, but I think your painting is very good,' de Silva said as they ate.

'That's decent of you. I wish more people agreed, but this isn't New York or Paris. Portraits are what people around here usually want.'

De Silva suddenly remembered where he had seen the man before. It was at the flower show at the Residence. He was the artist who had been commissioned to paint Archie's portrait. Today, however, in contrast to his flamboyant attire at the Residence, he was unremarkably dressed. 'People like the assistant government agent?' he asked.

A spoonful of kottu roti halfway to his mouth, the artist nodded. 'Yes. Do you know him?'

'He's my boss. At least for a little longer.'

'A good chap, even if he thinks painting has been going downhill since the time of Gainsborough.'

De Silva laughed. 'It's not a subject we have ever discussed.'

'My name's Tranter, by the way. Laurence Tranter.'

'Inspector Shanti de Silva.'

'Anyway, the portrait's finished, and Archie and his wife seem happy with it. A commission I was offered afterwards is also done, and nothing else has come along, but I like this part of the world. I think I'll stay a few weeks. Paint some more pictures. Who knows? Someone might buy them, and if they don't, I've had a good time. If I stay long enough, perhaps I'll even organise an exhibition.'

'I think you would find that popular,' said de Silva, thinking he might see if Jane would come and have a look with him, perhaps even buy a new picture for Sunnybank.

'You're very kind.' Tranter finished his meal and stood up. 'Thanks for the company. I'd better get back to work. The light goes very quickly here.'

De Silva nodded. 'Thank you too for your company. I must also get back to work.'

They wished each other goodbye, and as he returned to the Morris, de Silva recalled that Tranter's commission after Archie's portrait had been to paint Venetia MacDonald. De Silva wondered if he had any idea that she had disappeared. But then, why would he? It wasn't common knowledge, at least not yet.

CHAPTER 5

The sun was going down as he turned off the main road onto the narrower one that led to Waverley. On the way it had occurred to him that he should have stopped off at the police station before he left town to telephone Jane. It was unfortunate but now Hebden's request would have to wait until he got home.

Where the road forked, a signpost directed visitors to the left for the plantation's factory and offices and to the right for the house itself. He took the left fork and soon the factory sheds with their tin roofs came into view. Work had presumably stopped for the day; groups of workers were headed in the direction of a huddle of mud-roofed huts that must be their accommodation. When he drove into the main yard, a man was padlocking the tall metal doors of the nearest factory shed. De Silva asked where he might find William MacDonald's secretary and was directed to a building on the far side of the yard.

'You can go home if you've locked everything up, Akash,' he heard a woman's voice call out as he approached the entrance. 'I'll be here a while longer.'

'It's not Akash, ma'am,' he said, putting his head around the door. 'I am Inspector de Silva of the Nuala police. I presume you're William MacDonald's secretary.'

'Yes, my name's Geraldine Fraser.' The tall, elegant young woman's dark hair was pinned up in a neat style. She wore a tan skirt and a cream blouse with a softly draped bow at the neck.

'I'd be grateful if you would spare me a few minutes of your time.'

'What's this all about? Douglas told me William was suddenly taken ill. That's dreadful news. When he was here yesterday morning he seemed perfectly well. He left before lunch and didn't return, but since he and Venetia got married, he doesn't always work the long hours he used to. I assumed they were spending the rest of the day together.'

So, there was no point asking her where William had been yesterday after he left the plantation.

'Is there any more news of William?'

'He's still in hospital at Hatton. They believe he suffered a heart attack but thankfully help came in time and he has a good chance of recovery.'

'Is Elspeth with him?'

'Yes.'

'Douglas also told me Venetia is missing. At a time like this, it seems odd to leave the house without telling anyone where she was going. He wondered if I'd seen her today, but I haven't. He was off to look for her with some of the workers. Do you know if they've found her yet?'

'I understand not.'

So, Douglas hadn't mentioned Elspeth's accusation. Did that mean he didn't believe it?

'You will let me know if there's anything I can do, won't you?'

'Of course.'

Geraldine shook her head sadly. 'What a terrible situation. Please tell Elspeth I'll see to it that everything that needs to be done here is dealt with. And tell her my thoughts are with them all. I'll pray for William's speedy recovery and Venetia's safe return.'

* * *

De Silva returned to the fork in the road and took the turning that led to the house. When it came into view, it looked even more forbidding than before, with its dark bulk crouching beneath the fiery colours of the sunset sky. He knocked at the door and after a short pause, a servant answered and went to fetch Pamu.

'Good evening, sahib,' he said. 'I'm afraid I have no news for you, and the search has been called off until morning. It would be too difficult in the dark. Your sergeant has also gone home.'

De Silva nodded. 'I understand.' Under other circumstances, he might have felt it his duty to insist that the search went on, but he was beginning to doubt that Venetia was still on the estate.

'I need a photograph so that posters can be made to help in our search.'

Pamu looked hesitant.

'I have Memsahib Elspeth's permission.'

The servant's brow cleared. 'Very well, sahib.' Pamu led de Silva to a drawing room where many family photographs were arranged on top of a grand piano. He selected the most suitable one. 'And now, I'd like to take a look at Mrs MacDonald's rooms.'

'Very well.'

They had just returned to the hall when a man emerged from the next-door room. He bore a resemblance to William MacDonald but didn't have his athletic figure or air of good humour. De Silva guessed this was William's brother, Douglas.

'What's going on, Pamu?'

'This is Inspector de Silva, sahib. I was about to show him upstairs.'

'Good evening, Inspector. I'm Douglas MacDonald. A word before you go up.'

He turned on his heel and went back into the room he had emerged from.

'I don't know what you expect to find up there,' he said when de Silva followed him in. 'Your sergeant's already taken a good look. At a time like this, one might consider it an intrusion.'

Close to, de Silva smelled whisky and noticed that the whites of Douglas's eyes had a yellowish tinge. 'I have no wish to intrude, sir, but I would like to see for myself.'

Douglas gave a gruff snort. 'If you insist, you'd better get on with it. I expect Pamu's told you we've abandoned the search for my sister-in-law for tonight, but it will start again tomorrow at dawn. I hope I can rely on you to use every means at your disposal too.'

'Of course.'

'I suppose you know that my sister has a theory that Venetia tried to poison our brother.'

'And what's your opinion?'

'It's hard to believe that a lovely girl like that...' His voice trailed away and for a moment or two he seemed lost in his own thoughts then he rallied. 'But of course appearances can be deceptive,' he said briskly. 'Whether it's true or not, it's a relief that William's condition is improving. I was just on my way back to the hospital, so when you're done, Pamu will see you out.'

'Before you go, sir, may I ask what you were doing yesterday?'

'What do you need to know that for?'

'Merely to build up a picture of your family's movements over the day. I'm already aware that your sister was engaged with church business and your sister-in-law was out shopping.'

Douglas grunted. 'Very well, if you must know, I went into town and lunched at the Jockey Club. After that I socialised with friends there and played billiards. I returned home after William had been taken to hospital and went straight down there to see what was going on.'

'When you saw him at breakfast yesterday morning, did he say anything about how he planned to spend the day?'

'No, I assumed he would go to the plantation.'

De Silva made a note and thanked him, then they parted company.

Back in the hall, Pamu showed him up a grand staircase balustraded with carved mahogany. The wall on the left-hand side was hung with numerous photographs, including ones of William fishing or golfing, and Elspeth posing beside a variety of cars, sometimes proudly holding up trophies. He recalled David Hebden saying that she was an accomplished driver.

On the first landing they reached, they passed a door framed with a classical pediment. 'What's in there?' de Silva asked.

'It was the late sahib's study. Sahib Angus was a very learned man. He liked to study nature.'

'May we go inside?'

Pamu looked a little reluctant. 'Memsahib Elspeth doesn't like anything to be touched. She and Sahib Angus were very close. She often helped him in his work, and everything has been kept as it was when he died.'

De Silva smiled. 'Don't worry, I won't touch anything and if the memsahib notices that anyone has been into the room, you may say I was responsible.'

Pamu smiled. 'Thank you, sahib.'

The room was of medium size, cluttered with dark furniture and leather armchairs. The floor was covered with a burgundy carpet patterned with gold lozenges; red velvet curtains were half-drawn across the tall windows. Box frames containing butterflies and moths decorated the walls and in one corner of the room, a stuffed fox snarled in a glass case. The air smelled of must and beeswax.

Pamu gestured to a table laid out with small coloured glass bottles, lidded jars, corkboards, pins, and rolls of cotton wool. 'That is where the sahib worked preparing his butterflies and moths.' He lowered his voice. 'Many of us were sad that he killed them so that they could be displayed.'

'It makes me sad too,' said de Silva. 'Butterflies and moths are far too lovely to kill, and their lives are short as it is.'

They left the room and continued upstairs. Venetia's room was at the front of the house with a splendid view over the gardens. In contrast to her late father-in-law's study, it was filled with light, and prettily furnished with pieces in the chinoiserie style.

'Your sergeant searched very carefully,' said Pamu. 'He found nothing that would help us to know where the memsahib has gone to.'

'I'm sure he did. By the way, when Sahib MacDonald returned home yesterday, did he say anything about where he'd been?'

Pamu shook his head. 'No, he was taken ill very soon after he arrived.'

'Thank you, I think that's all for now. Would you send the memsahib's maid to me? I'd like a few words with her. I'll wait here.'

De Silva spent the intervening time investigating the room. He doubted Prasanna had missed anything, but it was best to check for himself. He looked into cupboards and drawers but there was nothing out of the ordinary in them. Venetia's jewellery box was on the dressing table, so he lifted out the trays and carefully ran a hand over the lining, but the sky-blue velvet was smooth to the touch.

He turned his attention to the bed, reaching under the mattress and patting down all the surfaces but there was nothing that might provide a clue. The elegant marble fireplace had apparently not been used for a long time;

there were no traces of ash in the grate and the back and side plates were shiny and unmarked by soot. If Venetia had been corresponding with an accomplice, she must have disposed of the evidence in some way other than by burning it.

He went over to the window and saw that the room overlooked the drive where Douglas was walking across to a cream Lagonda. All at once, he stopped and turned back to look at the house. De Silva thought he discerned something hesitant in his bearing, as if he might return, but then he seemed to change his mind, got into the car, and drove away.

There was the sound of footsteps in the corridor and the maid came into the room. Timidly, she gave him her name.

'Don't be afraid, you're not in any trouble. I just want to ask you a few questions. Have you worked for the memsahib since she came here?'

'Not for the first few weeks, sahib. Memsahib Elspeth chose her maid, but then Memsahib Venetia asked for me instead.'

Hmm, thought de Silva, *a spy in the camp*. Elspeth must have been annoyed about being thwarted.

'Memsahib Venetia is very kind,' the girl went on. 'She is never angry when I make a mistake.'

'I'm sure that doesn't happen often.'

'Oh, it did at first,' the girl said impulsively, then she gave de Silva a shy smile. 'But the memsahib always helped me to learn how to do my work in a better way.' Tears welled up in the girl's eyes. 'You will find her, won't you?'

'I hope so.' De Silva wished he could be more reassuring, but it was no use misleading her.

'Did your mistress ever seem unhappy?' he asked.

'She looked sad if Sahib MacDonald had to go away.'

'As far as you know, did she ever argue with Memsahib Elspeth?'

The maid's hands twisted in her apron. 'I'm not sure,

sahib.' She lowered her eyes and paused then murmured, 'Yes, perhaps there were angry words sometimes.'

De Silva suspected she knew perfectly well that there had been but was unwilling to be honest in case this conversation got back to Elspeth. The girl was probably afraid of her.

He let the maid go and went back downstairs to the hall. Pamu was waiting with the carefully wrapped photograph. De Silva took it and went out to the Morris. It was too late to organise the posters tonight. He would go to the office of the *Nuala Times* in the morning and ask for them to be printed. Now it was time he went home to Jane.

* * *

When he reached Sunnybank, Emerald's car was parked in the drive. Jane met him in the hall.

'Emerald came a few hours ago. She's out on the verandah, but I wanted a quick word with you before you say hello to her. She's told me about William being taken ill and Venetia's disappearance. She's terribly upset about it all. I hope you're bringing good news.'

De Silva bent down to stroke Billy and Bella who had also come to greet him. 'Some good, but some bad, I'm afraid. William's condition is improving although he's still heavily sedated, but the news concerning Venetia is far from good.'

'What do you mean?'

Quickly, he explained about Elspeth's accusation.

Jane's brow furrowed. 'Oh, Shanti, surely it isn't true.'

'I hope so as much as you do, and there's a younger brother who doesn't appear to be so sure of it, although he seems an odd character and hard to fathom. But the longer Venetia is missing, the harder it will be to dismiss the charge. Hebden told me that he wasn't completely convinced by the hospital's diagnosis. He examined William recently and found him to be in excellent health. He thought it conceivable that he had ingested poison of some kind, although he wasn't laying the blame at Venetia's door. It could have happened accidentally.'

'Should we say anything to Emerald? She's upset enough already. We know Elspeth doesn't like Venetia. She could easily be motivated by spite.'

'It's possible, but Hebden thinks Emerald can't be kept in the dark for ever. He won't be home until late and was hoping you would speak to her.'

Jane sighed. 'I suppose he's right. We shouldn't treat her like a child. We'd better get it over with.'

Emerald rose from her seat when de Silva and Jane joined her. 'Has she been found?' she asked anxiously.

'Not yet, I'm afraid.'

'Let's sit down,' said Jane. 'I'll call for some more tea. I expect Shanti would like a cup and so would I. What about you, Emerald?'

Emerald murmured something that might have been acquiescence and Jane rang for one of the servants.

'Where have you looked?' asked Emerald. 'Are you certain that every corner of Waverley has been searched? It's a huge estate.'

'The search was called off just before dark, but Douglas and the servants will start again at dawn.'

Emerald gave a little shiver. 'Do you think she's had an accident? If she was very upset last night anything might have happened. In the dark, there are so many hazards. That lake for example.'

Leela their servant came in with fresh tea and another cup and saucer. Tea, thought de Silva, as Jane poured it out, the universal British panacea. But he feared it would take more than tea to console Emerald when she heard what he had to say. He realised she had stopped speaking and was looking at him closely. 'Is there something you're not telling me?'

Jane cast him an apprehensive glance.

'I'm afraid there is. Elspeth MacDonald has accused Venetia of poisoning William.'

'What?' Emerald's eyes flashed. 'That isn't true.' Her voice rose. 'She's accusing Venetia because she hates her. She has done from the moment Venetia and William announced their engagement. I hope you don't believe a word she's saying.'

Jane put a hand over hers. 'Emerald, try to stay calm. I expect you're right, but Shanti has to investigate this all the same, don't you see?'

Emerald wiped tears from her cheek and gulped. 'I'm sorry I shouted, and I know you have to do your duty, but I promise you that Venetia doesn't have a bad bone in her body. She loves William and she'd never do anything to harm him. If he was poisoned, he must have taken something accidentally. When he recovers—' She stopped and put a hand to her throat. 'He will get better, won't he?'

'The hospital are confident that he will,' said de Silva.

A smile of relief warmed Emerald's expression. 'When he recovers, he'll be able to tell us exactly what went on, and everything will be alright.'

Her smile vanished as quickly as it had come. 'As long as Venetia hasn't come to harm.'

* * *

'Poor Emerald,' said Jane later when Emerald had gone home. 'Of course, I don't know Venetia as well as she does, but I trust her judgment. I'm sure Elspeth is extremely fond of her brother and that could be clouding hers. Is he really out of danger? I expect you didn't want to frighten Emerald.'

'Fortunately, he is, so I didn't need to dissemble. The signs are good.'

'That's something to be grateful for.'

'Yes, I just need him to recover sufficiently to answer some questions, but when that's going to be is in his consultant's hands.' He explained about Bradley-Clarke. 'Hopefully once he's satisfied, we can sort this tangle out.' He stretched. 'It seems a long time since my lunchtime snack in the bazaar.'

'I think cook is almost ready so we can eat soon if you like.'

'Good, then I'll leave my whisky until after dinner, but can I pour you a sherry?'

'Thank you, but not tonight.'

A few minutes later, Leela announced that dinner was on the table. De Silva put Bella down and was reprimanded by a few imperious flicks of her tail. 'I have to eat, you know,' he said, amused. 'I expect you had your supper hours ago.'

His spirits rose at the sight of steaming dishes of vegetable curries accompanied by brinjal relish, and spicy potatoes glistening with ghee. Even if he hadn't made a great deal of progress today, he intended to enjoy his meal.

'You said you've been up to Waverley,' said Jane. 'What's it like?'

'Grand but not at all attractive from the outside, although there are some impressive rooms.' He told her about what he'd seen of the house and more about his conversation with Douglas MacDonald.

'Waverley sounds very Victorian,' she said. 'Many people who had the money to build big houses in those days liked to copy the style of medieval times, at least what they thought the style would have been. I'm sure that in reality, medieval castles and grand houses were frequently draughty and dirty. Smelly, too, that's why people used to burn bunches of herbs to sweeten the air.'

De Silva helped himself to another serving of spicy potatoes. The rich colour of the turmeric they had been cooked with reminded him of the tawny wings of some of the butterflies and moths in Angus MacDonald's study. When, in between mouthfuls of potato, he told her about it, Jane shivered. 'I know that a lot of the Victorians were keen naturalists, so Angus wouldn't have been unusual. To be fair, without them the human race might not have progressed as fast in medicine and all kinds of things, but putting butterflies in jars and killing them doesn't seem to me to advance the progress of science a great deal.'

'I wholeheartedly agree.'

He cleared his plate and leaned back in his chair. 'Anyway, I've talked to Venetia's maid. She seems genuinely fond of her mistress, but I had the impression that the girl was afraid of Elspeth. She was cautious when I asked if Elspeth and Venetia ever exchanged cross words, but her reticence told me a lot.'

'Do you need to go back there tomorrow?'

De Silva shook his head. 'I have the photograph of Venetia that I need for the posters I want putting up. I'll get on with that in the morning. I plan to ask the editor at the *Nuala Times* to help me out. He's usually happy to do me a favour. I also ought to let Archie know what's going on. You know how rumours get around, and I don't want him hearing about the situation from anyone else.'

'Do you think he'll be inclined to believe Elspeth?'

'Hard to be sure, but somehow I doubt it. At the flower show, he appeared to be quite an admirer of Venetia's.'

'I must say, it's hard to believe that Emerald could be so wrong about Venetia. I know Elspeth claims to be certain she's guilty, but if she dislikes her so much it would suit her to say that whether she believes it or not. What if Venetia didn't run away? She and Elspeth both spent that first night William was in hospital at Waverley. Elspeth's obviously a resourceful lady. Might she had found a way of arranging for Venetia to disappear?'

De Silva considered the possibility. It would obviously be a convenient way for Elspeth to dispose of her rival. 'The problem with that idea,' he said at last, 'is that in the case of an accidental poisoning, Elspeth would have had almost no time to lay her plans. Even if she is resourceful, I think that spiriting Venetia away at such short notice on her own would be too much of a challenge.'

'Yes, but her brother Douglas might have helped. His scepticism about the accusation might be a front. After all, the alternative would be that she knew her brother was going to be poisoned by someone else, which seems extremely unlikely as he's such a popular man, or she somehow managed to poison him herself. Surely even to remove a rival she wouldn't risk her beloved brother's life?'

Or would she? mused de Silva. It was a shocking thought, but it was too soon to dismiss any theory. 'Suppose she found a way to give William a minute dose of poison. Enough to make him ill but not to kill him.'

'Do you really think she would have been prepared to take the risk of getting that right?' asked Jane, frowning. 'And when would she have done it?'

'I'm not sure. I haven't checked her alibi for the day William collapsed, although it should be easy enough to do so. She told David Hebden that she was at the vicarage all morning for a committee meeting and stayed for lunch. Might it be one that you participated in?'

Jane shook her head. 'Not that day. There are so many committees at the moment with Independence Day coming up.'

'That's a pity. I'd rather not arouse anyone's suspicions by asking questions.'

'What about Mrs Peters? She's always very discreet.'

'That's true. Maybe I'll have a word with her.'

'I think we need a rest from the case,' said Jane with a sigh. 'Perhaps things will become clearer tomorrow. Shall we listen to some more music after dinner?'

'Good idea.'

Dinner over, they returned to the verandah. On the way, de Silva poured himself a post-prandial whisky then chose a record. He put it on and went to join Jane.

As the gentle strains of Beethoven's Violin Concerto drifted from the drawing room, he felt the pace of his thoughts slow. As always, Jane's advice was sound. He should rest tonight and begin again tomorrow with a clear head.

CHAPTER 6

At the office of the *Nuala Times* early the following morning, a receptionist greeted him and dialled the editor's number on the internal telephone.

'Inspector de Silva is here to see you, sir, shall I tell him you're available?'

There was an unintelligible rattle of words from the other end of the line then she put down the receiver. 'He can see you now, Inspector. Would you like someone to show you the way?'

'Thank you, but I already know it.'

At the far end of the hall, he climbed the concrete stairs that led to the first floor. When he went through the door from the stairwell, he was met with a bustle of noise and activity. All along the corridor, voices and the clack of typewriters came from inside the rooms that lined it. Shirt-sleeved men hurried past him, shoes squeaking on the linoleum-covered floor. As he passed the print room, he heard the clatter of the presses and smelled ink.

The editor's office was at the far end of the corridor, his name picked out in curly gold lettering on the glass panel set in the upper half of the door. De Silva knocked and went in.

The editor was a middle-aged Sinhalese man whom de Silva had come to know quite well over his years in Nuala. 'Good afternoon, Inspector,' he said, getting up from his chair. 'What can I do for you?'

De Silva produced the photograph of Venetia from its package. 'I need two hundred posters printed from this picture. Can you help? The lady has gone missing.' He held out the photograph.

The editor nodded. 'Very pretty. What has she done?'

'As I say, she's missing, and I need to find her before she suffers a mishap.'

'And I suppose that's all you're going to tell me,' said the editor with a grin.

'I'm afraid I'm not at liberty to divulge anything more.'

'Well, I can do it for you, on the understanding that when the time's right, you give me an exclusive.'

'Willingly.'

'I suppose you want them as soon as possible.'

'Yes, please.'

'Do you have the wording?'

De Silva handed him the piece of paper he had torn out of his notebook and written on before he drove away from Waverley. The editor placed it alongside the photograph and studied them briefly. 'It looks straightforward. As usual, I'll do them for you at cost.'

'Thank you.'

'I'll tell my foreman to fit them in as soon as possible, so I should be able to let you have them later today. You're lucky we're not too busy with the evening edition. There's not much news in town at the moment. Everyone's preparing for the celebrations.' He held his hands wide apart in an expansive gesture. 'We'll be printing a grand souvenir edition to mark the day.'

'I look forward to it. If you'd telephone the station when the posters are ready, one of my officers will come to collect them.'

The editor nodded. 'I'll give him the invoice then.'

De Silva thanked him again and took his leave.

* * *

Nadar was alone at the police station when he arrived. Briefly, de Silva explained the latest developments in the case.

'William MacDonald is still in hospital at Hatton,' he continued. 'Get me the front desk there, would you? Maybe I can find out if there's any change in his condition this morning.'

'Yes, sir.'

The receptionist was helpful, and de Silva didn't have to wait long until a nurse came on the line. 'The patient is still under sedation, but Doctor Bradley-Clarke is confident that we can begin to withdraw the medication in the next day or two.'

'I'm glad to hear it. Do you happen to know if the test results from the samples that were sent to the laboratory have come in?'

'Yes, and the doctor said that if you rang, he'd like a word with you about them.'

There was another wait, a considerably longer one this time before Bradley-Clarke came on the telephone.

'Good morning, Inspector,' he said in a voice that radiated authority. 'The tests came back negative as I expected they would. Elspeth MacDonald has been informed, and I hope she's reassured, but if she's not prepared to let go of her idea, I leave it in your hands.'

'I understand. Can you give me any indication of when I might be able to speak to Mr MacDonald?'

'In a day or two perhaps. Someone will contact you.'

'Thank you.' He bade Bradley-Clarke farewell and went back to the public room where he gave Nadar the gist of the conversation.

'Is that good news about the tests, sir?'

'I'm not sure. Doctor Hebden mentioned they aren't

always dependable, and I doubt that Elspeth MacDonald will be easily convinced. I don't expect we've heard the last of her accusation. Where's Prasanna by the way?'

'He's gone to the bazaar, sir. We had a report of an argument between two stallholders that ended in blows, so he's gone to sort it out.'

'I see.'

Maybe he would make the short detour to the bazaar on the way to the Residence just in case Prasanna needed backup.

'I'll see you later,' he said to Nadar. 'As soon as a message comes from the newspaper to say that those posters are ready, go and fetch them. I want them distributed as soon as possible.'

* * *

The bazaar was quiet, and de Silva soon spotted Prasanna by a fruit stall talking with two middle-aged men. As he came closer, he noticed that they were speaking in Sinhalese. Both of the men looked rather hangdog, and one held a piece of bloodstained cloth to his nose.

'What have we here?' asked de Silva briskly as he reached them.

'There was an argument over the cart, Inspector,' said Prasanna, pointing to a small handcart nearby. 'These men are brothers-in-law, and they bought it together. Now one of them wants to sell his half.'

'And he wanted a price that would buy a whole fleet of carts,' said the man with the bloody nose.

'But you've agreed a price you're both happy with now, haven't you,' said Prasanna in a firm voice. 'You were just about to shake on it, and you've both assured me that you won't cause any more disturbance of the peace.'

Reluctantly, the man with the bloody nose held out his hand. His brother-in -law grudgingly took it and they exchanged muttered apologies.

'Right, we'll leave you to it,' Prasanna said. 'I expect you have work to be getting on with.' The two men nodded.

'Well done, Sergeant,' de Silva said as they walked to the Morris. 'You appear to have sorted that out satisfactorily. Keep an eye on the pair of them, of course. If there's any more trouble, we may need to levy a fine, but hopefully it won't come to that.'

'Thank you, sir, I will.' He grinned. 'I think that apart from the question of a price for the cart, there was some trouble between them because Deepak's wife, who is Ramesh's sister, was complaining to Deepak that he's lazy and doesn't work hard like her brother.'

'Ah, a family squabble. Well, let's hope it will blow over.'

They reached the Morris, and de Silva opened the driver's door. 'Hop in and I'll give you a lift back to the station.'

'Thank you, sir.'

As they wound slowly through the streets, avoiding handcarts pushed by bazaar traders, de Silva brought Prasanna up to date with the MacDonald case.

'Do you think Elspeth MacDonald might be right, sir?' asked Prasanna when he had finished. 'By the time I left Waverley yesterday, we had searched very carefully and there was no sign of Venetia. It's a long walk to any other houses, let alone back to Nuala, so if she didn't take a car—'

'It would be a reasonable assumption that if she's guilty, someone is helping her, as Elspeth claims, and she doesn't want to be found.'

They drew up in front of the police station. 'The editor at the *Nuala Times* has promised me that the posters with her photograph will be ready this afternoon. Between you and Nadar, get them put up around town and send a batch to the other local forces. I thought it best to describe her as missing rather than wanted. We don't want her aware that we suspect her of a crime.'

* * *

In the hope of catching Archie before he took his lunch, de Silva drove straight on to the Residence. At the front of the house, a team of gardeners was at work, some of them weeding the flowerbeds and others mowing grass or removing stray leaves from the pond around the fountain. A brass band was practising, the musicians' instruments gleaming in the sunshine as they played a rousing tune. As de Silva parked the Morris and climbed out, the piece finished and a young horn player changed the mood with a haunting lament. De Silva paused to listen, thinking how the two pieces encapsulated his feelings about what awaited his country: a mixture of eager anticipation and hope for the future, tinged with a modicum of nostalgia for the past.

On the way to the entrance portico, he noticed three men by the flagpole, busy checking that the ropes were running freely. A wise precaution, he thought. Important not to have any hitches when the new flag was raised on the big day.

Florence was in the reception hall, looking uncharacteristically flustered.

'Hello, Inspector, I mustn't stop to chat. So much to do. The celebrations are barely a week away. How everything will be ready, I can't imagine.'

De Silva smiled. 'I'm sure the day will be splendid, ma'am.'

'Oh, I do hope so.' She gestured to the staircase where de Silva saw a new painting hanging at the top of the first flight of stairs. It was the portrait of Archie.

'Such a relief it's finished in time,' Florence continued. 'It's a good likeness, don't you agree?'

De Silva studied the portrait. Tranter had made Archie a little handsomer than he really was, and somewhat more svelte, also accentuating the magisterial side of Archie's character at the expense of the humorous twinkle that often lightened it, but de Silva supposed that was the aim of an official portrait. He dutifully echoed Florence's opinion.

'I expect you've come to see my husband,' she went on. 'You'll find him in his study.'

De Silva thanked her and set off on the route that he had travelled so many times before. He wondered whether he would still do so after independence. Presumably, the Residence would continue to be used by the new government for some purpose but exactly what that would be was unclear.

He reached Archie's door and knocked, waiting to hear his boss's voice before he went in. Lady, Archie's black Labrador now grown from an excitable puppy into a calmer and mostly well-behaved dog, got up from her place by her master's chair and trotted over to greet him, tail wagging. He stroked her silky head then she returned to Archie's side and lay down again.

'Ah, de Silva, that was well timed. I'll be off in a few moments for lunch.' Archie gave him a wry smile. 'I expect I'll be eating alone. Lady and I are keeping out of the way. It seems the best course of action at the moment. Did you meet my wife on your way in?'

De Silva nodded.

'Then I expect she showed you the portrait. I was glad to get it over with. Decent enough chap, Tranter, but sitting for him wasn't my idea of fun. Rather be outdoors. But when the suggestion came up, Florence was very keen. I believe Tranter does quite a line in these official portraits. I suppose they're something to be remembered by.'

For a moment, de Silva thought that his boss's eyes looked a little misty. Independence would mean a big change in his life too. However Archie, with his dog and his love of outdoor pursuits, might come to terms with it more easily than Florence. She would have to find a new sphere in which she could be queen bee.

'What have you got for me today?' Archie was asking. 'I hope preparations are coming together satisfactorily at your end.'

'All in order, sir.' De Silva was glad that he had already been far enough ahead with them to say so with a clear conscience. 'But I'm afraid a problem of a different nature has come up.'

Archie harrumphed, and Lady raised her head from her paws and looked up at him with a worried expression.

'How serious a problem?'

Archie listened carefully as de Silva explained about William's sudden collapse, Venetia's disappearance, and Elspeth's accusation.

'Thank goodness Bill's out of danger,' he said when de Silva had finished. 'Have you spoken with him?'

'I'm afraid not. His consultant Doctor Bradley-Clarke is adamant that he mustn't be questioned yet. He's keeping him under sedation for another day or two.'

'I expect that particular problem will resolve itself but, if necessary, I may be able to have a quiet word and speed things up for you. What to make of Venetia's going missing and Elspeth's claim, I don't know, but my inclination is to disbelieve Elspeth. I find it very hard to credit that a delightful woman like Venetia has it in her to do anyone harm. Do we have anything else to help us?'

'Samples of William's blood and urine were sent for testing, but they came back negative. However, I understand from Doctor Hebden that one can't rely unquestioningly on that as some poisons are impossible to detect.'

'So I hear.'

'A plausible explanation for Elspeth's accusation might

be jealousy. Apart from any personal resentment she might feel towards a rival for her brother's affection, William has apparently changed his will so that Venetia stands to inherit the bulk of the Waverley estate. Before the marriage, it was presumably left between Elspeth and the other brother.'

'Ah yes, Douglas. The black sheep of the family. Has he an opinion on this accusation?'

'He seemed prepared to consider it but not as forcefully as his sister.'

'Interesting, especially as he probably stands to lose money in the same way that she does.' Archie paused. 'The more I think about it, the more I'm convinced this poisoning business is a piece of jealous meddling on Elspeth's part. One thing I am sure of is that the first person Bill will ask for when he recovers is Venetia. We need to have an answer for him, hopefully one he'll want to hear.'

'It's occurred to me that Elspeth may have taken advantage of the situation to arrange for Venetia to disappear.'

'That's a very serious accusation, de Silva.'

'I know, sir.'

Archie sighed. 'I suppose it has to be considered.' He frowned. 'The key thing is to find Venetia. That should give us the answers, so make it your top priority. What steps have you taken so far?'

De Silva explained about the posters.

'I assume you've made it clear to the editor that there must be no reporting of this?'

'Naturally.'

'Good. Keep me informed, won't you? And wrap it up quickly. The MacDonalds are a popular couple, and we certainly don't want anything to overshadow the celebrations.'

'I'll do my best, sir.'

As he returned to the Morris, de Silva sighed inwardly. Archie's reaction was an all-too-familiar one when a potential scandal involving the British threatened to become public, especially at an important time like this. As for Venetia, Archie might be right about her, but charm and good looks were not automatically proof of innocence.

* * *

An agitated Nadar met him when he reached the police station.

'Elspeth MacDonald has telephoned four times, sir. She says she must speak to you.'

'Did she say what about?'

'I'm sorry, sir, she wouldn't tell me.'

De Silva frowned. This was likely to be another awkward conversation. 'I'll go to my office,' he said, heading for the door. 'Get her for me now, please. Has Prasanna gone out?'

'Yes, sir, the *Nuala Times* telephoned to say that the posters you ordered are ready.'

Then until Prasanna was back, he had better not send Nadar to fetch him something to eat. His stomach was grumbling, but it would have to wait.

A few moments later, the telephone rang on his desk. He picked up the receiver. 'Miss MacDonald for you, sir,' said Nadar.

'Thank you.' He inhaled deeply. 'Good afternoon, ma'am. I understand that you wanted to speak to me urgently. I'm sorry I wasn't here when you called earlier.'

'Has my sister-in-law been found yet?'

'I'm afraid not, ma'am, but we are doing our best.' He explained about the posters.

'A pointless exercise,' she said irritably. 'The last thing Venetia will do is show herself in public. I doubt, however, that she has the wit to stay hidden on her own and now I've had time to consider it, I have a good idea who's helping her.'

De Silva waited.

'Laurence Tranter, the man who painted her portrait. They were very friendly, far too friendly to my way of thinking. It occurs to me that there may have been something between them in the past and they resumed the relationship when they met in Nuala.'

De Silva wasn't at all sure whether to take her accusation seriously. It smacked of a convenient surmise, but he supposed he had no choice if he didn't want to fuel her anger. As it was only yesterday that he'd met Tranter and he'd said he planned to stay for a while, it shouldn't be too hard to find him. Perhaps someone at the Residence would know where he was staying. He decided not to mention the meeting to Elspeth. She might construe it as an attempt to dismiss her theory by implying that, far from acting suspiciously, Tranter was going about his business in a normal fashion.

'Very well, ma'am,' he said. 'I'll try to find Mr Tranter and question him. And please let us know how your brother progresses. My officers can take a message or, if the station is closed, you are welcome to telephone my home.' He gave her the number. In a slightly mollified tone, she thanked him then ended the call.

When he returned to the public room, Prasanna was coming through the door carrying two cardboard boxes piled one on top of the other. He had something wrapped in brown paper tucked under one arm.

'The posters, sir.'

'Good.' De Silva pointed to the counter. 'Put them down there and I'll take a look.'

Prasanna placed the boxes on the counter and, removing the package from under his arm, laid it next to them. 'That's the photograph, sir.'

De Silva joined him and lifted the flaps on the first box. The smell of printer's ink wafted to his nostrils.

'The foreman said they did their best to dry them quickly, sir.'

De Silva took one out and studied it. The photograph of Venetia had transferred well, and the text was clear.

'I want plenty of these put up around town. You'd better lock up here so you can both do the job. Divide what you don't need into bundles and take them to the railway station. I want them on the afternoon train with instructions to leave some at every stop. Nadar, you can telephone the local police in advance to let them know they're coming. Send the largest consignment to Hatton. I'll give Inspector Singh a call myself. I have to go out to see a man called Laurence Tranter.' He explained briefly who Tranter was. 'Elspeth MacDonald has got it into her head that he's in league with Venetia MacDonald and helping her to avoid being found. I'm not convinced she's right, but we need to be seen to be investigating all avenues.'

* * *

After he had made a brief call to Inspector Singh, de Silva telephoned the Residence and asked to be put through to the office. Luckily, they had the address of the hotel that Laurence Tranter was staying at. De Silva recognised the name. It was a respectable establishment.

A stop at the bazaar on his way there involved a detour, but de Silva decided that the demands of his stomach were more urgent than a visit that was probably going to prove fruitless. He hadn't bargained on a delay, however, and forced to wait in a queue of trucks, carts and rickshaws, he tapped the Morris's steering wheel, half regretting that he hadn't decided to postpone his meal until after he had visited Tranter's hotel.

When the traffic moved on, half a dozen elephants appeared up ahead. A good-looking young man with black curly hair who wore a scarlet tunic stood at the roadside, waving vehicles on. The drivers edged carefully past the huge animals; no doubt aware that one flick of their trunks could do considerable damage.

'What's going on?' asked de Silva as the Morris drew level with the young man.

'The mahouts are getting their elephants used to the crowds.'

De Silva refrained from asking why this exercise had not been cleared in advance with the police. The intention was good. The prospect of elephants running amok during the celebrations was an alarming one.

He drove at a snail's pace, taking his turn to pass the creatures. The largest one, a bull, walked at the front, close enough for him to reach out to touch it. Its leathery hide rippled and when the Morris drew level with its head, a red pinprick eye surveyed him and its huge ears flapped. Beads of sweat broke out on de Silva's forehead, but at a command from the mahout, the elephant settled back to a steady pace. Relieved, de Silva drove on.

Twenty minutes later, fortified by dahl, rice, and a glass of fresh mango juice, he made his way to the hotel. It was a pleasant-looking building with walls painted a sunny yellow and green shutters at the windows. Two well-fed looking dogs dozed in the shade of the front porch. One of them raised its head and thumped its tail as de Silva passed by.

The cool lobby with its checkerboard-tiled floor and whitewashed walls was deserted. De Silva rang the bell on the desk and was about to ring it again when the bead curtain hanging at the door opposite the entrance rattled and parted. The man who appeared greeted him apologetically. De Silva suspected he had been asleep.

'What can I do for you?' he asked.

'I'm looking for an Englishman called Laurence Tranter. I believe he's staying with you.'

'He was here for a few weeks, but he left early this morning.'

De Silva frowned. That was a sudden change of plan. 'Did he say where he was going?'

The manager shook his head. 'I don't think so, but he may have told my deputy manager who was here yesterday.' He went to the curtained door and called out. Shortly afterwards, a younger man appeared. De Silva asked the same question, but the young man couldn't help him.

'Did Tranter have a car?' he asked.

'No,' said the manager. 'When he wanted to go anywhere, he asked someone to call him a rickshaw.'

'Was that what happened this morning?'

The young man nodded.

'Might the rickshaw man remember where he took him?'

The young man shrugged. 'The rickshaw man was only passing by. He doesn't take our guests regularly.'

De Silva sighed inwardly. There were hundreds of rickshaw men in Nuala.

'I'm sorry we can't be of more help,' said the manager. 'Sahib Tranter is a popular man. You're the second person today who has asked about him.'

'Really? Who was asking?'

'He didn't give a name.'

'Can you describe him to me?'

'A local man, about your age.'

'He had a moustache,' said the younger man.

That described a lot of men in Nuala, de Silva thought wryly. He thanked them for their help and went back outside. He wondered who the moustached man was. This unexpected turn of events changed his view of Tranter. Had he left suddenly to join Venetia? It was galling to think that after all, Elspeth might have found the key to the mystery.

* * *

Outside the hotel, although it would mean returning after dark, he decided to take the photograph of Venetia back to Waverley. He was also interested in seeing the portrait of her that Tranter had painted. First, however, he would drop in at the British clubs in town and also the Crown Hotel. They were all places where William might have lunched on the day he collapsed. He might as well visit them now and get those enquiries out of the way.

As he passed the church, he noticed a line of cars parked outside. A funeral must have taken place, for groups of people in sombre clothing were walking down the path to the lychgate or standing in little knots on the grass verge, engaged in conversation. One group in particular caught his attention. Two ladies, both tall, clad in black, and veiled were talking with the vicar, Reverend Peters. There was something vaguely familiar about them, but he had still failed to place them when they shook Peters' hand and parted. One of them took her companion firmly by the arm and helped her along the path, stopping only briefly when other mourners wanted to talk to them.

Parked just outside the lychgate was a black Bentley with a uniformed chauffeur in attendance. When the ladies reached it, he held open the rear door. They got in and were driven away. As the car disappeared from sight, de Silva continued to wrack his brains. For some reason that he couldn't put his finger on, it seemed important to know who they were, but in the end, his efforts to identify them remained fruitless.

* * *

At the British clubs he was told that William hadn't been in on the day in question. His brother Douglas had, however, lunched at the Jockey Club as he had claimed and spent the afternoon there playing billiards. The club's manager thought he left at about six o'clock.

De Silva moved on to the Crown and asked to see his friend Gunesekera, the manager.

'Forgive me for keeping you waiting,' Gunesekera said when he arrived. 'I have a very busy day. In fact, all days are busy at the moment. We'll be full for the celebrations, and everything needs to be perfect. This afternoon I have a dozen things to do from going over banqueting menus with the head chef to making sure enough brandy and whisky has been ordered.' He paused and gave de Silva an apologetic smile. 'But I'm sure you too have many extra burdens to shoulder. How is everything going?'

'According to plan, thank you, and it's as well it is, because just at the wrong time, something has come up.'

'I take it this is something I may be able to help with?'

'Yes, I'd like to know if a man called William MacDonald has been a guest here.'

'William MacDonald? He certainly has. He comes here often, either with his wife or with friends or business acquaintances. He's a charming fellow. He treats the staff well, no matter what their rank, and tips generously.'

'Did he lunch here the day before yesterday?'

'That's easy enough to find out for you, but why do you ask?'

'Because I'm afraid he was taken very ill later in the day.'

Gunesekera raised an eyebrow. 'I hope you're not suggesting that the hotel's food was at fault. I take our reputation very seriously.'

'Of course not, it would just be helpful to know who he was with that day. He might have mentioned something about feeling unwell, or about his activities earlier in the day.'

'I'll ask the head waiter. Would you like to wait in the lounge?' He pointed to the open door.

'Thank you.'

The lounge was a pleasant room with rosewood furniture and sofas covered in yellow silk. A pile of magazines lay on a coffee table, so he sat down, picked one up and glanced idly at it to pass the time. The picture on the front cover showed the British king and queen in their crowns and bejewelled and bemedalled finery. The aloof expressions on their faces reminded him of waxworks. It was strange to think that soon their sway over his island would be largely ceremonial.

They had visited Ceylon once. He had been a sergeant in the Colombo police at the time. He remembered how leave had been cancelled and much of the force had been out on the streets manning the barricades along the processional route from the docks to Government House. The visit had been a brief one; Ceylon had never been as important to the Empire as its much larger neighbour, India.

'The last time William lunched here was a week ago,' said Gunesekera on his return. 'His wife was with him and a few friends. I can give you their names if you wish.'

'Thank you, perhaps later.'

'I suppose you can't tell me more about what's going on.'

By now Prasanna and Nadar should have some of those posters up, so he needn't keep Venetia's disappearance quiet, thought de Silva, even though it was best not to tell his friend the rest of the story.

'It's no great secret. I'm pleased to say that William is on the mend, but we are very concerned about his wife. Understandably, she was extremely distressed by his sudden illness, and now she's missing. If you hear anything, I'd be grateful if you'd let me know.'

'I'll keep my eyes and ears open. I hope you find her soon, also that William fully recovers. It must be a very anxious time for the family.'

'Are you acquainted with the rest of them?'

'His brother Douglas used to come in here, but we haven't seen him for a few months. There was some unpleasantness over his account, but eventually William settled it. There's also a sister, Elspeth. She lunches here occasionally. I fear she can be as abrasive as William and Venetia MacDonald are charming. On several occasions, I've been forced to intervene when a meal hasn't been to her liking. Even some of the restaurant's most experienced waiters have been reduced to jelly.'

De Silva chuckled. 'I'm sure you do a good job of smoothing things over.'

Gunesekera shrugged. 'I hope so. The British and their problems, eh? Still, I don't suppose they'll be our concern for much longer. When we both have time, we must have a drink and a good old chinwag about what the future holds.'

CHAPTER 7

It was nearly dark by the time he turned in to the drive at Waverley. He drove straight up to the house and parked on the immaculate gravel sweep in front of it alongside the cars that were already there. The lights at the front of the house revealed a sporty Morgan two-seater, a black American Cadillac, and a maroon Austin, modest in comparison with its expensive neighbours.

There was no sign of any of the outside staff. With the package containing the framed photograph of Venetia under one arm, he rang the doorbell and waited, then when a servant opened the door, asked to see Pamu.

'Please come in, sahib,' said the servant. 'I will fetch him.'

De Silva stepped into the cavernous hall. After the warm air outside, he felt a chill. He wondered if William, by all accounts such a sociable man, ever wished he had not inherited such an old-fashioned, eccentric place. He was fairly sure that a young lady like Venetia would prefer something more modern and cheerful. He was just considering what that might be when the sound of footsteps snapped him back to attention. This wasn't the slap of a servant's soft-soled shoes; this was the click of a woman's high heels. For a moment, he felt a surge of anticipation. Had Venetia returned, and if she had, how would she account for her absence?

'Inspector de Silva! I wasn't expecting to see you here.'

Geraldine Fraser, carrying a folder under one arm, seemed flustered. 'Is someone attending to you?'

'Thank you, they are. A servant has gone to fetch Pamu. I'm afraid I have no news of Venetia, but I'm delighted to say that the report from the hospital about William is encouraging.'

An expression that de Silva couldn't read passed across Geraldine's face, then she resumed her mask of professional calm. 'Yes, so I've heard. Elspeth telephoned to let us know. She sounded very relieved. Have you been able to speak to him yet?'

It was a natural enquiry, and he couldn't put a finger on his reason for reading more into it, but instinct told de Silva that Geraldine was concealing something.

'Not yet, but I hope it won't be much longer before he's well enough.'

Geraldine glanced over his shoulder. 'Ah, here's Pamu coming now. I'll leave you with him. I have a few matters to deal with before I finish for the day.'

As the front door closed behind her, he greeted Pamu and held out the package. 'I've come to return Memsahib Venetia's photograph.'

Pamu took it with a smile. 'Memsahib Elspeth telephoned from the hospital to tell us that the master is much better.'

'That's excellent news, isn't it? Have you continued to search for Memsahib Venetia today?'

Pamu shook his head. 'No, Sahib Douglas said we had done enough, and everyone must get back to work.'

'Is he here?'

'He left after lunch saying he was going to the hospital.'

'I see.'

'Is there anything else I can do for you, Inspector?'

'If Memsahib Venetia's portrait is in the house, I'd like to have a look at it.'

If Pamu thought it was a strange request, he gave no indication.

'It's hanging in the dining room. I will show you.'

De Silva followed him down the panelled corridor hung with gilt-framed oil paintings of Scottish lochs and glens that led to the dining room. Pamu turned on the electric light to reveal an imposing room, the lower part of its walls panelled in the same dark wood as the corridor and the upper part decorated with garnet-coloured wallpaper patterned with gold fleurs-de-lys. A long mahogany table with fourteen chairs around it ran down the centre of the room. Antique porcelain tureens painted with fruits and flowers stood at intervals on the table's highly polished surface, and between them were pairs of silver pheasants.

A huge mirror with a scrolled gilt frame hung over the black marble fireplace. There were several portraits of distinguished-looking gentlemen and ladies in Victorian or Edwardian dress, then in marked contrast, the portrait of Venetia.

She wore a sky-blue gown with thin, diamanté-encrusted straps that set off her slender shoulders. A pearl choker was fastened at her throat by a sapphire the size of a hummingbird's egg and her blonde hair was elegantly styled in soft waves. Despite her finery, however, or perhaps because of it, there was something lifeless about the portrait. The dress and jewellery had been painted with great flair, but her expression lacked the vivacity that de Silva had admired when he saw her at the Residence on the day of the flower show. He knew that instinctive reactions were unlikely to impress Elspeth MacDonald, but his told him that this wasn't a portrait painted by a man in love.

He took out his notebook. 'When did Sahib Tranter finish the portrait?' he asked Pamu.

'Only a few days ago.'

'Would that be before or after your master was taken ill?'

'Before.'

'Whose job was it to see to it that he was paid for his work?'

'Mine, Inspector. He had already received the money before the master was taken ill.'

So Tranter hadn't remained in Nuala to get his money. It made his assertion that he was staying on because he liked the area seem genuine. If Elspeth was right, he had suddenly changed his plans with the purpose of helping Venetia to get away, but somehow, de Silva doubted that.

He thanked Pamu and went back outside. The maroon Austin 7 was no longer there. Presumably, it belonged to Geraldine.

* * *

He drove home more slowly than he had on the way to Waverley, enjoying the warm night air. It was too early for the moon to be up, but the sky glittered with stars. At the brow of the hill that overlooked Nuala, he paused to admire the view. Skeins of lights twinkled brightly where houses and streets were lit by electricity; in other places, a soft glow showed that the only lighting was from oil lamps or candles. In the middle of town, where the bazaar was situated, there was a pool of darkness. Stallholders and customers would have gone for the night leaving the place to scavengers such as stray dogs and cats, or the wild creatures that only emerged after dark.

He wanted to go home and talk to Jane, but decided to call in at the station first in case Prasanna and Nadar were still there and there was any news. They would have had time to put up some posters and the ones that they had put on the train might also have been distributed.

Both their bicycles were chained up outside and they were talking in the public room.

'Good evening, sir,' said Prasanna. 'We weren't sure if you'd come back today, but we thought we'd stay on a while in case you did.'

'Thank you. I've just been up to Waverley to return that photograph. Are the posters up around town?'

Prasanna nodded. 'And the bundles for the train have gone too. Nadar and I telephoned the other police stations between us.'

'Good. No calls from them yet, I suppose?'

'I'm afraid not, sir,' said Nadar. 'But there have been several from Elspeth MacDonald. She's still at the hospital and wants you to telephone her.' He looked uncomfortable. 'She talked about speaking to Mr Clutterbuck if she doesn't hear from you soon.'

'I'm sorry, sir,' added Prasanna. 'We've tried to reassure her, but it's not easy.'

'I'm sure you have. Never mind. You'd better get the hospital for me now and ask them to track her down.'

He had only been settled in his office for a few minutes when the telephone rang.

'Miss MacDonald for you, sir,' said Nadar.

'Thank you, put her through.'

'About time,' Elspeth snapped. 'Have you found Tranter yet?' De Silva held the receiver away from his ear. Elspeth's tone was as cutting as barbed wire.

With a sinking feeling in his stomach, he explained that he had visited Tranter's hotel and been told the man had left with no forwarding address.

'There!' said Elspeth triumphantly. 'What more proof do you need?'

'I appreciate you're very concerned about catching whoever may have endangered your brother's life, ma'am. I share that concern, and I assure you that every effort will be made to trace Laurence Tranter, but we mustn't lose sight of the fact that if he's left town, it may be a coincidence.'

'I have no faith in coincidences, Inspector. It surprises me that you do.'

The line went dead, and de Silva sat still for a moment, attempting to compose himself. He realised that the hand which had not been holding the receiver had been so tightly clenched that the marks of his nails had imprinted themselves into his palm. He should not let Elspeth affect him so deeply. She wasn't the first person to be angry at the time it took to solve a case, and she most certainly wouldn't be the last. Perhaps it was tiredness that made him more sensitive than usual. He took his handkerchief from his pocket and wiped his forehead then went out to the public room. Prasanna's and Nadar's expressions were apprehensive.

'I'm afraid the lady was not impressed when I had to tell her that Laurence Tranter has left Nuala, and the manager of the hotel where he was staying had no forwarding address.'

'Do you think she's right about him, sir?' asked Nadar.

'I'm keeping an open mind, but it would be good to find him.' He raised an eyebrow. 'If only to convince her that we have our eye on the ball.' He looked at his watch. 'You two had better get off home now. I'll have a think about what we might do to track down the elusive Mr Tranter.'

* * *

As he drove home to Sunnybank, the unpleasant conversation with Elspeth hung about him like a rank smell that persisted after he had let himself into the house and hung his jacket and cap on the hook in the hall. It was quiet, so assuming Jane was outside, he went to find her. On the threshold of the verandah, he paused. She was sitting in her chair, engrossed in a book. Close by, Billy and Bella were curled up on the wooden floor fast asleep. The scene was a picture of domestic harmony. The memory of the day's tribulations fading, he smiled. How lucky he was to be happily married and enfolded with love: how lucky to have his little family.

Jane looked up. 'Hello, dear.'

'I'm sorry I'm late.' He stepped onto the verandah and went to sit in his chair then bent to stroke the cats who had woken and come to greet him.

'Have you already eaten?' asked Jane.

'No, I wasn't particularly hungry, but I expect you are.'

'Only a little.'

She looked at him sympathetically. 'Was it a bad day?'

'I've had better.'

She listened thoughtfully as he told her about it.

'I find it hard to believe that Elspeth's right about Venetia and Tranter,' she said when he had finished. 'Emerald is so convinced that she's happy with William, and I've never known her to be mistaken about people. But what do you think?'

'I'd be more confident that we can rule out Elspeth's accusation if Tranter hadn't suddenly left his hotel this morning without mentioning where he was going. With so much going on, I forgot to tell you that I met him in the bazaar at Hatton yesterday after I'd visited the hospital. I went to buy a snack for lunch, and he was there painting. He struck up a conversation with me and mentioned that he liked the area and intended to stay on for some time, even though he'd finished his portrait commissions.'

'I agree it seems odd that he's changed his mind so soon.'

'He may have a reason that has nothing to do with the MacDonalds, although his haste suggests it's not an innocent one. All the same, I think it's important to find him and hear what he has to say for himself.'

'If he is involved, it would be interesting to know if he's been in touch with the hospital, perhaps calling anonymously from a public telephone, to find out if William has recovered. Tranter may be afraid William will tell us something that incriminates him.'

De Silva rubbed his chin. 'Yes, and the same would apply to Venetia. I haven't actually enquired whether anyone has been asking after William, and I must. Oh, another thing I forgot to tell you, the hotel manager said someone had already come looking for Tranter today, but he didn't get their name and could only give me a brief description. A local man about my age with a moustache.'

'Not a great deal of help.'

'No.'

'Is there anything else you can think of?'

'Yes, although I admit it's no more than a hunch. I went up to Waverley to return the photograph we used to make the posters about Venetia being missing. Whilst I was there, I had a look at the portrait that Tranter painted of Venetia. It was well done, but I didn't get the impression that it was anything more than a work painted on commission, and there was merely a casual acquaintance between the artist and his sitter. Of course, I didn't tell Elspeth that. I doubt she'd be impressed. As for Tranter, finding him isn't likely to be easy. At the moment, I have nothing to go on, not even a photograph of him.' He sighed. 'I think this is shaping up to be what your Sherlock Holmes would have called a two-pipe problem.'

'Perhaps they could help at the Residence. There might have been a little ceremony when Archie's portrait was unveiled. You know the kind of thing.'

'Do you mean a photograph taken together to mark the occasion? That's a good thought. I'll call now. Hopefully, Archie will be available.'

'Whilst you're doing that, I'll tell cook we're ready for supper.'

'No luck,' he said when Jane returned. 'Archie and Florence are out at a dinner. It will have to wait until morning.'

CHAPTER 8

After breakfast, de Silva's first call was to the vicarage. 'The memsahib is in the garden,' said the servant who answered the door. 'Shall I show you the way?'

'Thank you, I think I can find it for myself.' De Silva felt he knew Mrs Peters well enough by now to dispense with being formally announced. She was as fond of her garden as he was of his and on occasion, there was even a little amicable rivalry between them.

He took the path that ran along one side of the house and found her with her gardener inspecting the damage to the netting of a fruit cage. Suddenly, a harsh cry came from the far side of the lawn, and she looked up.

'Good morning, Inspector!' She gestured to the peacock and peahen near a bamboo clump. The peahen continued to peck away at the grass, but her mate had fanned out his iridescent tail feathers and was turning slowly from side to side. 'Fred is as good if not better than any guard dog. Unlike Ginger who's usually more interested in finding insects.' She turned back to her gardener. 'You may get on with your work now.'

The gardener nodded and walked off.

'May I offer you a cold drink, Inspector?'

'That would be most welcome.'

'Then we'll go and sit on the verandah. I'm afraid if it's the vicar you want to see, he's out at the moment visiting a parishioner. Her husband died, and the funeral was yesterday. My husband would usually wait a while to discuss the arrangement for the gravestone, there's only a temporary marker at the moment, but the widow insisted she wanted to get on with having it made, so she asked him to visit her today.'

'Actually, it was you I wanted to talk to, ma'am.'

'Ah, I hope I can help, but let's make ourselves comfortable first.'

As they walked towards the house, Fred must have decided that he had done his duty for he lowered his tail feathers. 'The netting on our fruit cage should have been repaired by now,' Mrs Peters remarked, 'but after the heavy rain we had the other night, the soil was too wet to walk on. I was just telling our gardener I want him to get on with the job today. I feel a little sad about depriving the birds, but our gooseberries and raspberries are so delicious.'

'I'm sure the birds can find plenty of other things to eat.'

'I hope so.'

De Silva followed her up the steps to the verandah, admiring the jasmine that clambered up the columns supporting the roof, its tiny white trumpet flowers filling the air with perfume. Mrs Peters told a servant to bring fresh lemonade and she and de Silva chatted about the garden until the servant brought a jug of it, poured out glasses for them and then departed.

'Now, what can I do for you?' asked Mrs Peters.

'You may have heard by now that William MacDonald was recently taken very ill.'

Mrs Peters nodded. 'I had heard something about it. I hope his condition is improving.'

'Slowly, although it's unfortunate that it's not yet possible to ask him any questions. The hospital take the view he suffered a heart attack, but as he's normally in robust health, Doctor Hebden is of the opinion that he may have eaten something that caused his illness. I'm trying to find out what that might have been, but so far, I've been unable to establish where he was and what he might have consumed that day. He left his office at the plantation before midday and by the time he arrived home he was already in a parlous state. Naturally, his family's primary concern was to obtain medical help.'

'Of course, but haven't they been able to tell you anything?'

'No, William's sister Elspeth last saw him at breakfast and tells me she spent a large part of the day here. She only returned to Waverley after he had been taken ill.'

'Yes, she was here. We had a committee meeting that lasted all morning. Afterwards, some of the ladies, including Elspeth, stayed to lunch.'

'Do you recall what time she left?'

Mrs Peters gave de Silva a shrewd look. 'I'm sure you have a good reason for asking me. I won't ask what it is. I remember the exact time. It was ten minutes to four. I had to go straight over to the church for a choir rehearsal. I was playing the organ.'

De Silva knew that as well as being a keen gardener, Mrs Peters was an accomplished musician.

'What about his wife Venetia?' she went on. 'Can't she give you any information?

'I'm afraid I've not had the opportunity to ask her. By the time Doctor Hebden alerted me that there was a problem, she had gone missing.'

Mrs Peters frowned. 'How strange. I hope she hasn't got into any trouble.'

'One thing is for certain and that is she appeared to be very distressed.'

'I'm sure she was. Oh dear, I wish I could help, but I can't claim to know her well. I've no idea where she might go for help or to whom she would turn. I doubt it would be her sister-in-law. I'm afraid that Elspeth seems to harbour considerable antipathy towards her.' Mrs Peters lowered her voice. 'She's not the most charitable of people, but then it must be hard to adjust to a new state of affairs. She was in charge at Waverley for so many years. What's been done so far to find Venetia?'

'Posters have been put up in town and sent to all the towns down the line. Other than that, the estate at Waverley has been thoroughly searched.'

'We must all pray that she's found unharmed.'

* * *

At least he knew that Elspeth had been telling the truth about her movements, thought de Silva as he left the vicarage. He decided to go on to the golf club as it was the only one of the clubs that the British frequented where he hadn't yet enquired about William's whereabouts on the day he was taken ill.

A short while later he turned into the driveway, and soon the clubhouse with its imposing entrance and tall sash windows rose up before him. Scarlet canna lilies grew in the flowerbeds on either side of the portico, like rows of flames against the whitewashed walls.

As he drew to a halt, de Silva felt the twinge of discomfort that he often did when he had to visit places like this where the membership was exclusively British. He had no desire to play golf, and suspected that few of his countrymen did either; cricket was the game that most of them loved. It was hard, however, not to resent being shunned in one's own country, even though he usually managed to adopt a philosophical attitude to things he could do nothing about. No doubt the situation would change once Ceylon was independent, but that was for the future.

'Good morning, de Silva!'

He turned and saw Archie. He was dressed for golf in a tweed cap, shirt and tie, and plus-fours with woollen socks and sturdy shoes. 'What brings you up here?' he asked.

De Silva's heart sank. He knew that since Archie wanted him to focus on finding Venetia, his errand was unlikely to go down well. As he feared, when he explained, Archie scowled. 'I thought I'd made my views clear.'

'You did, sir, but I still believe it's important to establish where William was on the day he was taken ill.'

There was a long pause, then to de Silva's surprise, the scowl faded. 'Very well, I suppose we might as well not make this a wasted journey. Although I doubt the club will be happy if they think you're suggesting there might have been something amiss with the food here, and we've already agreed that it's best if no one knows there's any question of something being suspicious about his illness. I'll tell you what—'

He waved to his caddy who waited a little way off with a bag of golf clubs. 'Go to the first tee and tell my companions I'll be along in a few moments,' he shouted then turned back to de Silva. 'You stay here. I'll go in and make up some excuse for wanting to know if Bill was here.'

'Thank you, sir.'

Archie returned a few minutes later, his sturdy shoes crunching over the gravel. He shook his head. 'He wasn't here. Anything else to report?'

'I'm afraid Elspeth MacDonald is becoming very impatient.'

Archie nodded. 'You don't surprise me.'

'She's also claiming that Laurence Tranter is involved.'

'What? The painter fellow?'

'Yes, she's suggesting that he and Venetia have been having an affair, and conspired to poison William.'

'Good grief! What does she base that on?'

'She says they got on suspiciously well when Tranter painted Venetia's portrait. Elspeth also claims to have heard her making clandestine telephone calls.'

'Hardly conclusive. A charming woman like Venetia knows how to get on well with people. As for these clandestine calls, she might simply have been aware that Elspeth was spying on her and felt uncomfortable.'

'I'd agree with you, sir, if it wasn't for the fact that Tranter left Nuala early yesterday morning. The hotel where he was staying hadn't been expecting it and he left no forwarding address. I also happened to meet him the previous day and he told me that he intended to stay on in the area for a few weeks. Why would he bother to move hotels locally?'

'Perhaps he wasn't comfortable at the hotel.'

'I doubt that would be the case. The place has a good reputation.'

Archie groaned. 'I suppose one has to admit it may put a different complexion on the matter. As I've said, this couldn't have come at a worse time. What's the news of Bill?'

'He's improving steadily.'

'Hmm, which could explain why both Venetia and Tranter have made themselves scarce. Hopefully, once it's possible to question Bill, we'll be able to find out the truth. Well, I'd better be getting on with my game. We'll have to talk more about this later. Keep me informed.'

'Of course, sir. Oh, and before you go, it would be helpful to have a photograph of Tranter. I wondered if there might be one at Residence.'

Archie scratched his chin. 'I seem to remember my wife organised something when that dratted portrait was unveiled – is that how one describes it? She and I had to stand next to the thing with Tranter and smile whilst a chap with a camera buzzed around. Your best bet is to call my office. They'll probably be able to help.'

* * *

As he drove to the police station, de Silva's mind went back to the Elspeth. If William's collapse had not been caused by a heart problem, there were two possibilities: either that he had been deliberately poisoned, or that the poisoning had been accidental. In the former case, if Elspeth was behind it, she would have had ample time to work out what to do with Venetia, but Mrs Peters had confirmed that Elspeth had been at the vicarage on the day in question, so she had lacked the opportunity to poison William even if she had wanted to take the risk. He ruled that out. If, on the other hand, Elspeth had taken advantage of an accidental poisoning, she would have needed to make an impromptu plan. He decided that, as Jane had suggested, in that event she must have enlisted Douglas's help. Where would they have taken Venetia? Even somewhere remote on the plantation would attract considerable risk, so they might have found a way to move their captive to an even more out of the way place. It seemed that Elspeth had hardly left her brother's side since he was admitted to hospital, so Douglas would have needed to do the job.

De Silva remembered the sporty, low-slung MG that Hebden had pointed out in the hospital car park. However good the driver, it would never be possible to negotiate anything but properly made-up roads in it and the same would apply to the other cars he had seen parked outside Waverley. But what about the plantation vehicles? They would need to be sturdy to cope with the tracks through the tea fields, and no doubt Douglas would be able to get hold of one of them with very little trouble. It would be worth going back to the plantation to take a look around and ask some more questions.

With a shudder, he considered the possibility that to ensure Venetia was never found, Elspeth and Douglas might have decided to murder her.

* * *

Nadar was alone when de Silva arrived at the police station.

'Sergeant Prasanna has gone out to make sure that all the posters we put up in town are still there, sir,' he said when de Silva enquired where he was. 'In case any of the local children decide to play a trick and take them down.'

'A commendable precaution. Has he been gone long?'

'A little over an hour, sir.'

'I need a word with the office at the Residence. Get the number for me, would you? I'll take the call next door and explain to you what this is about when I've spoken to them.'

The official at the Residence agreed to look out the photograph and have it ready for de Silva, who went back to the public room to speak to Nadar.

'I'm going up to the Residence to collect a photograph they have of Laurence Tranter. He may already have left Nuala but if you show it around at a few places, the railway station for example, someone might recognise him. If Prasanna gets back before I do, fill him in, please.'

* * *

De Silva returned with the photograph an hour later. It showed Archie, Florence, and Tranter standing next to Archie's portrait. Florence appeared to be enjoying the occasion, although Archie looked about as comfortable as a bull on a tightrope.

Prasanna had come back and was talking with Nadar, but they stopped at the sight of de Silva.

'Nadar has explained everything to me, sir,' said Prasanna. 'We've been listing the places we can try.'

'I leave it to your discretion.' He handed Prasanna the photograph. 'Here you are. I'd like you to cut away the part that shows the Clutterbucks. It would never do for anyone to make a connection between them and the search for Tranter.'

'What shall we say if anyone asks why we're looking for him, sir?'

De Silva cast about for an idea. 'Say he left without paying his hotel bill. Now, one last thing before you go, Nadar. Get me the hospital in Hatton. I want to find out if anyone has been asking about William MacDonald's progress.'

The receptionist who answered the call had only been on duty for a few hours. Twirling his pencil between his thumb and forefinger, de Silva waited for a few moments whilst she spoke with some of her colleagues.

'Apparently, a lady who didn't give her name rang yesterday evening, but no one who's on duty at present remembers any other callers.'

That was interesting. Could it have been Venetia? If it was, she must have access to a telephone and that suggested that she wasn't being held somewhere against her will.

'Was she given any information?'

'I'm afraid the person who spoke to her isn't on duty until later, but I can ask her when she comes in.'

'Thank you. Is Miss MacDonald still with her brother?'

'Yes, she hasn't left his side. She insists on her meals being brought to her, and she sleeps on a camp bed the nurses put up.'

'What about Mr MacDonald's brother?'

'He visited yesterday afternoon.'

He thanked the receptionist for her help and rang off, then sat for a moment considering what to do next. Deciding to go to Waverley to find out about the vehicles that were kept on the plantation, he went out to the public room and was halfway to the door when the telephone rang. He picked up the receiver. Hebden was on the other end of the line.

'De Silva? I expected one of your chaps to answer.'

'I've sent them both out to look for Laurence Tranter, the fellow who painted Archie's portrait.'

'What do you want him for?'

De Silva explained about Elspeth's latest accusation and Tranter's unexpected departure.

'I think I'll hold off telling Emerald about this. It will only add to her distress. Personally, I find it hard to believe the allegations Elspeth's making. Emerald and I have seen quite a bit of Venetia and William since they married, and if she only married him for his money and is unfaithful, I'd be very surprised. It's not unusual for extreme circumstances to affect a person, and possibly Elspeth believes what she says, but I'd say there's a distinct chance that she's lying.'

'What do you think about Tranter's unexpected departure?'

'Could be a coincidence he's moved on. After all, a fellow can change his mind. I've not come across many artists, but perhaps the artistic temperament is more prone than others to making sudden decisions. On the other hand, arguing against myself, if he's involved with Venetia and they plotted to kill William, he would be alarmed if he knew that there was a chance of William recovering, very likely leading to them being unmasked.'

'I've just learned that a woman who didn't give her name telephoned the hospital to ask after William yesterday evening. I'm not sure what information she was given, if any, but the receptionist is trying to find out.'

'If it was Venetia, it suggests she's not a prisoner.'

'Quite.'

Hebden paused a moment. 'Well, all things considered, I stand by my opinion that Elspeth has invented the whole story. Although that doesn't answer the question of why Venetia has gone missing.'

De Silva hesitated then decided to mention his suspicions about Elspeth and Douglas.

'I'm sure they'd be glad to see the back of Venetia,' said Hebden when he had finished, 'Elspeth in particular, but it would be a very risky thing to do. And where would it end? Are you suggesting they'd resort to murder?'

'I'm not sure, but it's something I have to consider.'

'Phew! I sincerely hope you turn out to be wrong.'

'Likewise.'

'I was actually ringing you because I've been thinking more about those test results. Despite Bradley-Clarke's view, I'm still not convinced we ought to rely on them. Tests provide the answer in many situations, but they're fallible. How do you feel about my speaking to the friend I told you about? The former director of the Botanic Gardens. He may be able to help in some way.'

'Thank you, I'd be very interested to know what he has to say.'

'I'll see what I can do.'

De Silva thanked him and ended the call then, taking out his notebook, and jotted down the details of the conversation. When he had finished, he went out to the Morris. Although he had never harboured great hopes of a positive result from the laboratory, it would have made his life a great deal easier if he knew for sure that William had been given poison and what it was, but perhaps Hebden's friend would be able to offer useful advice.

* * *

The road to Waverley was becoming familiar, so he took his eyes off it more readily to admire the hilly green tea terraces that unfolded on either side of him. Small figures of tea pickers moved amongst them, their backs bent under the large panniers into which they tossed the freshly plucked leaves. He felt a pang of sympathy. Tea gathering must be gruelling work, especially with the hot sun beating down. These workers were by no means the poorest in Ceylon, but their pay was meagre. Would their lot improve when the island was independent? It was more likely, he thought sadly, that they would be far back in the line for new opportunities and a better life.

He turned left at the fingerpost and soon arrived at the factory. There was much more activity than there had been on his previous visit. Workers were unloading leaves from carts and taking them into a long, low building that must be the drying shed. He wondered if Geraldine Fraser was in her office. He would go and talk to her before he left. It would be interesting to see how she received him. There had been something strange in her manner the last time they met. First, however, he wanted to find out about the vehicles used to get around the plantation.

He stopped a passing worker and asked to be taken to whoever was in charge. The man pointed to the long building. 'That is Sahel, sahib. He's in the drying shed.'

De Silva followed him in and paused on the threshold. After the bright sunshine outside, his eyes took a moment to adjust to the dim light. The air was thick with heat and the scent of tea. He blinked as fine dust drifted into his eyes; the sound of voices and machinery, amplified by the low ceiling and bare walls, made his ears throb.

The worker who had shown de Silva in pointed to a man standing beside one of the drying tanks, his nose buried in a handful of tea leaves. As he scattered them back into the tank and dusted off his hands, he noticed de Silva and walked briskly over. 'Can I help you, Inspector?' he shouted.

'I hope so.'

Nodding to the man who had brought de Silva to him, Sahel told him to get back to work then led de Silva to his office. It was a small room with a high window filmy with dust. The walls were mostly racked out with shelves but brightly coloured posters portraying steaming cups of tea set against backgrounds of smiling workers on green hills filled some of the empty spaces. A large, felt-covered board crisscrossed with webbing bristled with letters, invoices, and orders.

Sahel pulled up a chair for de Silva then sat down on the opposite side of the desk. He had a pleasant face with a broad nose, wide mouth, bushy eyebrows, and receding grey hair.

'What can I do for you, Inspector? I hope you bring good news of Sahib William. It has been an anxious time.'

'I'm glad to say that I do. The doctors say his condition is steadily improving.'

'This is indeed good news. But has Memsahib Venetia been found?'

'Not yet, I'm afraid, but everything possible is being done to find her.'

Sahel looked gloomy. 'I don't know how we can help. Pamu told me that he and his men have searched everywhere.'

'I'm sure they have. We think she must have left the plantation, but all the cars at the house are accounted for. Might she have taken a vehicle from down here? Something Sahib William would use to drive around the plantation for example?'

'I don't think any of them are missing, but if you wish I will show you.'

De Silva thanked him, and they went out by a side door and through a maze of buildings to a yard where two jeeps were parked. Both were painted khaki, and one was open topped, but the other had a canvas roof and side flaps. A more likely choice if one wanted to transport someone in secret. He went closer and studied it. The windscreen was extremely dirty and there was mud on the wheels and splashed up the sides and radiator grille. Many dead insects were smattered on the headlights. He straightened up and turned to Sahel. 'When was this one last driven?'

'I'm not sure. It is normally Sahib William who uses it.'

'Someone's driven it on a very muddy road. Would that be him?'

'I don't know,' said Sahel awkwardly. 'It should have been cleaned and not left in such a bad state, but it wasn't drawn to my attention.'

'I see. Thank you for showing me. I don't think I need detain you any longer.'

De Silva set off to find Geraldine Fraser. As he walked, he mulled over what he'd seen. The state of that jeep was interesting. The last time he remembered very heavy rain falling was the night that Venetia had disappeared.

* * *

He didn't need to go as far as Geraldine's office for he saw her drive into the main yard. She brought her car to a halt next to her office door, and climbed out, seemingly in a hurry to go inside. He wondered if she hadn't noticed him, so he called out her name. She looked over and when she saw who was calling her, gave him a polite smile. 'Hello, Inspector. Are you looking for me? I'm sorry I wasn't here. I had a few errands to run. I hope you're bringing me good news.'

'I'm afraid there's still no progress with finding Venetia, but the hospital is happy with the improvement in William's health.' He paused. 'But perhaps you already know that. I believe a lady telephoned the hospital to enquire. Was that you?'

There was a perceptible hesitation before she spoke. 'No, I'm not a member of the family. I would have liked to call but I thought that they wouldn't give me any information. I've no idea who it would be.' De Silva wondered if he imagined a fleeting defensive look in her eyes. 'But I'm so glad that William is getting better,' she went on. 'Will you be able to talk to him soon?'

'I expect so.' De Silva watched her face for a reaction, but the mask didn't slip. He wondered what was going on behind it. Shouldn't a loyal secretary simply be pleased to hear that her boss was out of danger? The obvious reason for that not to be the case was that she feared what would happen if he recovered. Was she hiding something? An idea started to incubate in the back of his mind.

* * *

It was late afternoon, so he decided to go home. Jane's car was parked in the drive, and he found her in the drawing room putting the finishing touches to a flower arrangement. He recognised delphiniums from the garden.

'I hope you don't mind. They looked so pretty that I asked Anif to bring a few in for me.'

'Of course not. I'm glad you like them.'

He had grown them from seeds given to him by Mrs Peters after he had admired them in one of the vicarage's borders. '*They're an English cottage garden plant*,' she'd said. '*I wasn't sure if the Ceylonese climate would suit them, but they've turned out to be very adaptable.*'

'Am I too late for tea?' he asked.

'Of course not.' Jane stood back and considered her arrangement. 'I think that will do. Why don't you go and sit on the verandah, and I'll have some brought out.'

'Good. I'll have a wash first. I feel rather dusty.'

He left his uniform jacket in the hall and went to the bathroom where he washed his hands and splashed his face, enjoying the soothing feel of the cool water on his eyes, still a little gritty from the dust in the drying shed at Waverley.

He picked up the comb that he kept on the shelf above the basin and pulled it through his hair, then feeling much better, went out to the verandah. Billy and Bella, who had come to the bathroom to see what he was doing, followed him. They settled down to snooze together in a patch of shade.

'David Hebden called me,' said de Silva after he had told Jane about his visit to the vicarage. 'Even with the tests coming back negative from the laboratory, he's still of the view that William may have been poisoned rather than having a heart attack. He's offered to speak to a friend of his who is a former director of the Botanic Gardens. Apparently, he's very knowledgeable about poisons and may be able to suggest something that would help us.'

'That's good, dear. Did you tell David what Elspeth said about Venetia and Laurence Tranter?'

'Yes, he wasn't impressed, and I'm inclined to agree with him although I'd still like to know what Tranter's up to. I went back to Waverley this afternoon. I was interested to find out what vehicles there are on the plantation. If Venetia was kidnapped, one of them might have been used to take her away. I suspected it would need to be something sturdy.'

'And did you find one?'

'I found two. A pair of jeeps, but one of them was much dirtier than the other. It may not mean anything, but I recall that it rained very hard on the night Venetia disappeared. If the jeep was taken out then, it might have been driven on muddy roads. Whilst I was at Waverley, I also visited Geraldine Fraser, William's secretary.'

'I don't think you've mentioned her to me before.'

'No, probably not. I met her the first time I went up to Waverley the day after William collapsed. She'd already heard he was ill, and was relieved to know that he had a good chance of recovery. All in all, she seemed very capable and wanted me to assure the family that she would cope.'

Jane paused to sip her tea. 'So why are you telling me about her now?'

'Because the next time I saw her, she seemed distinctly uneasy, even though the news about William continued to be encouraging. When I saw her today, I had the feeling she was hiding something.'

'I agree it's strange, but perhaps she has something else on her mind.'

'Considering how serious his condition was when he was first taken into hospital, I think it would have to be something quite major.'

'Yes, I suppose it would. I see your point. Perhaps she's someone else to consider.'

'A woman who wouldn't give her name telephoned the hospital to ask how William was progressing. Geraldine denied it was her, but we have no way of knowing if that's true.'

'But why would she want to harm William, or Venetia for that matter?' asked Jane.

'Geraldine's a very attractive woman. I'm not sure for how long she's worked for William, but during that time I expect they spent a fair amount of time in each other's company.'

'Are you suggesting there was something between them? A fling perhaps, that came to an end when he met and married Venetia?'

'It's crossed my mind.'

'The revenge of a spurned lover? Don't you think that's rather too dramatic?'

De Silva shrugged. 'Maybe, but I ought to consider it.'

'No stone unturned?' Jane asked with a smile. She lifted the lid of the teapot and looked inside. 'Would you like another cup?'

De Silva shook his head, and she picked up the milk jug. 'Then Billy and Bella may as well have what's left. It's been out here for too long to keep for another time.' She poured the milk into her saucer and carefully set it down on the wooden floor. Billy and Bella uncurled themselves and padded over.

'On the other hand,' mused Jane, 'if Geraldine was a spurned lover bent on revenge, it gives her a plausible motive. And if William was with her at his office that morning, she had an opportunity. It would be easy enough to slip something into a mid-morning cup of tea.'

'It would indeed.'

'It still leaves the possibility that Elspeth and Douglas took advantage of the situation to harm Venetia. Had Geraldine been responsible for her disappearance, she would have needed to know where Venetia was that night, and got into her bedroom at Waverley to abduct her without being noticed. I doubt she would have managed that.'

'A good point.'

Jane picked up the licked-clean saucer, and Billy and Bella miaowed expectantly. 'No more,' she said in a firm voice.

CHAPTER 9

At the police station the following morning de Silva found the station door locked so he left the Morris and set off on foot for the bazaar. The streets were busy with early deliveries. Smells of cooking came from open doors, and women with baskets of laundry under their arms walked in the direction of the place where the townsfolk did their washing at an open-air culvert, chatting and laughing as they went. At the corner of an alley, de Silva saw a black cat crouched against the wall. Its green eyes watched him warily as it snatched up the scrap of fish it had been eating and fled. He thought of Billy and Bella. Of course they had no idea how fortunate they were to have such comfortable lives.

Eventually, he saw Prasanna ahead. He was talking with a couple of men. De Silva walked over to them.

'Hello, Sergeant. How are you getting on?'

'These men work in this part of town making deliveries. They haven't seen anyone who looks like Tranter, but they'll come to the police station if they do.'

'Good.' De Silva nodded to the men.

'You may go about your business now,' Prasanna said.

'Anything else to report?' de Silva asked when they had gone.

'No, sir, but Nadar should be back in a minute. I said I'd wait for him here. Perhaps he'll have done better than I have.'

'I'll wait with you.' It would give him the opportunity to bring Prasanna up to date with the news about William and, for good measure, his thoughts about Geraldine Fraser. Prasanna listened attentively. 'Would you like me to try to find out more about her, sir?' he asked when de Silva had finished.

'How do you propose to do that?'

'When I was up at Waverley helping with the search, Pamu told me a bit about the people who work for the family. I thought it might come in useful.'

De Silva nodded approvingly. 'Good thinking, Sergeant.'

'He mentioned that Geraldine only started to work at Waverley about a year ago. Before that she was employed by a British company in town. I wrote down the name. Perhaps I could speak with them?'

'By all means have a word with them and see what they have to say about Miss Fraser, but I think it can wait for the moment. The important thing is to find Laurence Tranter. Ah, here comes Nadar. From his expression, my guess is that he hasn't come up with anything new.'

* * *

De Silva sent Nadar back to the station to keep an eye on things whilst he and Prasanna spent the rest of the day patiently trawling the local bars and small hotels with no success. By late afternoon, his feet were sore, and his temper frayed. He sent Prasanna home and went briefly to the station where Nadar had no news for him. He let him off duty too and set off for home.

At Sunnybank, Jane was in the drawing room working on a piece of embroidery. 'I decided to come inside,' she said. 'There seems to be a particularly large number of insects and moths about tonight.' She put the embroidery to one side. 'Tell me how you got on.'

'Prasanna and I must have visited every hotel and bar in Nuala, but no sign of Tranter, or Venetia for that matter. I must admit, my hopes weren't very high.'

'But you had to try,' said Jane. 'You mustn't be discouraged. I'm sure something will come up.'

De Silva flopped down in his chair and sighed. 'Under normal circumstances, I wouldn't be. The investigation hasn't been going on for very long, but with the big day coming up, there's more pressure to resolve it as quickly as possible. Archie's very keen it shouldn't detract from the celebrations. The ideal situation would be for us to find Venetia unharmed and establish that William is a victim of an accidental poisoning that no one's to blame for, but I'm not confident that's what will happen.'

He bent to stroke Bella. She narrowed her eyes and rubbed her cheek against his wrist. He was reminded of the black cat in the dark side street with its scrap of fish. 'I expect you've had a good day. Where's your brother got to?'

'Probably in the garden,' said Jane. 'He never minds insects. In fact, he seems to enjoy it when we have plenty around.'

Their servant Leela appeared in the doorway. 'Cook says dinner is ready, memsahib.'

'Thank you, Leela. We'll come through.'

'I feel better already,' said de Silva as he surveyed the table. 'Pea and cashew curry twice in one week, these delicious little vegetable samosas, green beans with coconut and what's this?' He pointed to a bowl of butter-yellow rice studded with quarters of hard-boiled egg and pieces of smoked fish, liberally garnished with chopped parsley. The smell of cardamom and cumin rose to his nostrils.

'Kedgeree. Florence was talking about it, and I realised that we've never eaten it at home, so I explained to cook how to make it.'

De Silva grinned. 'Ah, yes. A British imitation of our

food. As far as I can remember, I've never eaten it anywhere, but I'm willing to try.'

He served himself with some. 'Not bad,' he said when he had eaten a mouthful. 'But it could do with being spicier, and compared to our Ceylonese dishes, it's a little dry.'

'Oh dear, but you must have some more, or cook will be offended.'

'As I'm hungry, I certainly will, perhaps a dollop of yoghurt will improve it, but it hasn't changed my opinion that where British food is concerned, the only thing they cook better than we do is puddings.'

Jane laughed. 'Do you include Yorkshire pudding in that claim?'

De Silva put his head on one side. 'Hmm, the pudding that is eaten with roast beef?' He had been faced with the dish several times at the Residence and out of politeness eaten a small amount of the meat even though as a Buddhist he preferred not to. The pudding wasn't bad, crispy, and light, not unlike a roti.

'I believe I do.'

'So, what do you plan to do next?' asked Jane.

'Enjoy my dinner.'

She raised an eyebrow. 'You know what I mean.'

'Of course I do. Oh, I forgot to tell you that Prasanna came up with a good idea.' He explained about Prasanna's suggestion for finding out more about Geraldine Fraser. 'Now that we've exhausted our searches in town, I'll let him get on with it. It's always important to encourage initiative. Perhaps he'll unearth a lead, but otherwise, I'm mainly pinning my hopes on William fully recovering and shedding light on what happened to him.'

'As the time when that's likely to happen gets closer, it will be interesting to see what Elspeth does.'

'It certainly will.'

Shall we have some music after dinner? It might help

you to relax. We could listen to more Chopin or Beethoven, or would you prefer Debussy?'

'Debussy sounds a good idea.'

* * *

For once, however, Debussy's *Moonlight Sonata* failed to soothe de Silva. In bed, after a few hours of restless sleep, he decided to get up for a while. Moving quietly so as not to disturb Jane, he took his book and dressing gown and crept out into the passage. Billy and Bella must be sound asleep in the kitchen, he thought. Usually, when he got up in the night, they soon came to join him.

The air had cooled and the insects that had driven Jane inside were no longer in evidence, but there was still a low throb of cicadas. Fireflies glowed in the bushes. De Silva took a couple of cushions from the chest where they were stored overnight. He found a box of matches, lit the oil lamp on the table next to his chair, then carefully replaced the glass chimney over the flame. He watched it waver for moment before it began to burn strongly, emitting a soft light.

Satisfied that it wouldn't go out, he sat down and opened his book, but he hadn't been reading for long when a soft, beating noise disturbed his concentration. He glanced at the lamp and saw a pale blue moth fluttering against the glass. The proverbial moth to the flame, he thought. Perhaps he should extinguish the lamp in case it damaged its wings, but he was enjoying his book. It was Charles Dickens' *Great Expectations*. The setting was very different to anything he had experienced on his own verdant island, but that was part of what fascinated him. He was impressed by how vividly Dickens conjured up his native Kent marshes with their roaming sheep and lonely churches.

After a few more minutes of reading, a louder flapping sound drew his attention back to the lamp. To his dismay, he saw that the pale blue moth lay dead on the table, its wings crumpled like a scrap of dead leaf, but a magnificent Atlas moth had taken its place. Wishing he had saved its small cousin by blowing out the flame sooner, de Silva closed his book and swiftly did so, then watched the giant moth sail away into the darkness. He decided that he was beginning to feel tired enough to sleep and went inside.

Back in the bedroom, the mattress sagged a little under his weight as he got back into bed.

Jane stirred. 'Is something the matter?' she asked drowsily.

'No, I couldn't sleep, so I went outside to read for a while.'

'I hope you didn't get bitten.'

'No, it was fine. I'm sorry I disturbed you.'

'Never mind.' She rolled onto her other side and soon her breathing settled into a regular rhythm. In contrast he remained awake for another ten minutes thinking about the moths. It was strange how the answer to a problem could sometimes be suggested by a small, seemingly unconnected event.

CHAPTER 10

After his restless night, he slept for a little longer than usual, and Jane was already in the dining room when he arrived for breakfast.

'I didn't like to wake you,' she said. 'You looked so comfortable. Was it the case that kept you awake last night?'

'Probably. That and Mr Dickens, but my trip out to the verandah may have had an unexpected benefit.' He explained about the moths. 'I mentioned to you that one of the jeeps I saw at Waverley was very muddy.'

'Yes, and because of the rain, you thought it must have got that way on the night Venetia went missing.'

De Silva nodded. 'What I forgot to mention was that I noticed what looked like dead moths and insects on the headlights. After what I saw last night, it occurred to me that if someone was driving along in the dark, moths and insects would be attracted to the lights. It proves that the jeep was taken out at night.'

Jane frowned. 'Yes, it does seem to indicate that, but how does it help us to work out where the jeep went?'

'That's where something I remembered from a couple of months back comes in. It was in the nature notes column of the *Nuala Times*. I'm not sure if you read it but I believe I mentioned it to you. It was about a place out in the country where there's an abandoned tea plantation. The writer of the column saw a large number of Atlas moths there. The story stuck in my mind because I've never seen Atlas moths together in large numbers. If it had been a quieter time, I might have followed it up and tried to find the place to see it for myself. Perhaps I'm grasping at straws, but the article mentioned that it's a remote spot. I think it would at least be worth trying to find out who wrote the article, and talking to them.'

Jane thought for a moment then nodded. 'Yes, why don't you do that? It might lead somewhere.'

* * *

On the way to the police station, he stopped off at the offices of the *Nuala Times* and went in. The day was already heating up and fans were whirring.

'Back so soon?' asked the editor. 'If you've run out of copies of that poster, you may have to wait a few hours before we can run off another batch for you.'

'Thank you, but that's not why I'm here. It may seem an odd request, and you'll have to take it from me that I've a good reason for asking, but I'd like a word with whoever writes your nature notes column if they're available.'

'You intrigue me. I'm looking forward to the day when you're ready to spill the beans about what's really been going on. I hear a British lady is missing and it's rumoured that her husband has been poisoned.' He gave de Silva a shrewd look. 'I think there must be a pretty scandalous story there.'

'I can't possibly comment.'

The editor chuckled. 'I'm sure you can't. Well, to answer your question, the nature notes column is written by a young man called Guy Richardson. He's a keen naturalist, but the column's a side-line for him. His main job is at the Residence. I forget exactly what he does.'

De Silva jotted down the name in his notebook. 'Thank you, that's very helpful. I'll leave you to get on.'

'My pleasure. And don't forget,' he added as de Silva headed for the door, 'you owe me an exclusive.'

* * *

De Silva felt irritable as he drove to the station. With the posters on display, it would inevitably be common knowledge by now that Venetia was missing, but he wondered how the editor had found out about the poisoning allegation. Did someone at the hospital have a loose tongue?

He turned his mind back to the idea of investigating the abandoned tea plantation that Guy Richardson had written about, wondering if it was too farfetched. If he pursued the idea, as Richardson was an employee of the Residence, he ought to go through Archie to contact him and ask for his help in finding the way. He considered the possibility that Archie might think the idea was nonsense. On the other hand, he was anxious to bring the case to a conclusion, so perhaps he would be more willing than usual to agree to a speculative venture. The fact that he was obviously a great admirer of Venetia's might help too.

A commotion ahead abruptly brought his attention back to the road where a small crowd was gathered watching something. It was impossible to pass so de Silva brought the Morris to a halt and went to find out what the problem was. The crowd parted to let him through, and in a blaze of sunshine, he saw a cobra in the middle of the road, its hooded head swaying above its coiled body, its forked tongue flickering menacingly.

His skin crawled. He had never managed to conquer his fear of snakes, unfortunate when one lived in a country that was home to almost a hundred varieties of them. He knew that the creature was probably as much afraid of humans as he was of it, but snakes were at their most dangerous and likely to strike when they felt threatened. Angrily, he noticed a few stones around the cobra that had probably been thrown at it.

Careful to maintain a good distance between himself and the snake, he pushed through the onlookers, turned to face them, and raised his hands. 'Everyone back! Leave the creature alone. It may go of its own accord, but in case not, is there a snake catcher around here?'

People looked at each other and there was a general murmur of questioning. Eventually, an old man stepped forward. 'Dinuk, but he is not here.'

'Where would I find him?'

The man pointed to a side street. 'His house is down there. The one with the green door.'

It would probably be best to speak to this Dinuk himself, thought de Silva. 'Very well, I'll tell him to come and deal with the cobra.' He shook a finger at the onlookers. 'No one is to torment it whilst I'm gone, understood?' There were mutters of assent.

He soon found the house with the green door where he knocked and waited. He was just beginning to wonder if no one was at home when the door opened to reveal a scowling, sleepy-looking man rubbing bloodshot eyes. De Silva's sensitive nostrils smelled a whiff of arrack. It seemed to take the man a moment to notice his uniform, but then his demeanour changed to a much more obliging one.

'Forgive me, sahib, I was asleep. I had much work to do last night.'

De Silva doubted that it had been work that had kept the man up, but he went along with the fiction. 'Are you Dinuk?'

The man nodded.

'I hear you catch snakes.'

'Yes.'

'Then your help is needed.' Swiftly de Silva explained about the cobra.

'I'll fetch what I need and come.'

As he waited for Dinuk to return, out of the corner of his eye de Silva saw a movement, and something made him look closer. A tall woman in an olive-green sari was leaving a house at the far end of the street. The loose end of the sari was drawn over her head, also covering the lower half of her face. She cast a glance in his direction and hesitated for a moment before turning and hurrying off. The breadth of her shoulders and the way she moved looked odd for a woman. He wondered whether to follow but Dinuk had returned carrying a burlap sack and a long, stout stick with a loop of rope hanging from one end.

'Ready, sahib.'

'Do you know all your neighbours?' asked de Silva as they went back to where the crowd had assembled around the cobra.

Dinuk shrugged. 'Some of them.'

'What about the tall lady from the house at the far end on the same side as yours? The one with the terracotta-tiled roof? Dinuk shook his head. 'I don't know her, but the owner doesn't live there. He rents it out.' Dinuk rubbed an imaginary coin between his thumb and fingers. 'A rich man.'

'What's his name?'

A suspicious look came over Dinuk's face, but if he was curious, he must have thought better of asking why de Silva wanted to know. 'Ravindra, he owns the Golden Monkey bar.'

De Silva made a mental note to visit it as soon as the problem of the cobra was dealt with.

The crowd was still watching the snake, but he was glad to see that there were no more stones on the ground nearby. With impressive calm, Dinuk, who seemed to have shaken off his tiredness, had soon lassoed it with his pole. It writhed and hissed but he managed to drop it safely into the sack. Eyeing the squirming burlap with apprehension, de Silva gave him some money for his efforts. 'And take a rickshaw out of town and release the creature somewhere it won't cause trouble again,' he said. 'After that if you come to the police station, there'll be more money for you.' He gave Dinuk a piercing look. 'I don't want the snake killed, mind you, and I'll know if you're lying to me.'

* * *

Although he had never had occasion to visit the place, he recalled that the Golden Monkey bar was down a narrow alley, so he left the Morris where she was and went there on foot. At the bar, a closed sign dangled from the door; nevertheless, he knocked and waited. Eventually it opened and a man with a grubby cloth in his hand stood there. He looked too poorly dressed to be the owner.

'Tell them we're not open yet,' a deep voice called from inside.

'You're open to the police,' said de Silva firmly, stepping forward and ushering aside the man who had answered the door so that he could pass. Thankfully, it was a little cooler inside the bar than in the street.

'My apologies.' The words came from a pugnacious-looking man with a craggy face and muscular build who sat at one of the wooden trestle tables with which the bar was furnished. There were numerous papers on it, and the pen in his meaty hand hovered over one of them. 'What can I do for you?' he asked.

'Are you Ravindra?'

'Yes, I own this bar.'

'So your neighbour Dinuk tells me, and you also own a house in the street where he lives.'

'Dinuk?' Ravindra frowned.

'He is a catcher of snakes.'

'Ah yes, I know him.'

'I understand that you rent out the house. I'm interested in the lady who lives there at the moment. What can you tell me about her?'

A wary look came over Ravindra's face. 'She only took the room a couple of days ago. She didn't say much, but she paid the rent a month in advance.'

'Come on,' said de Silva impatiently, 'surely you asked for her name.'

'She told me it was Mrs Collins.'

'So she's British even though she wears a sari.'

Ravindra nodded. 'Sometimes British ladies enjoy dressing in local costume.'

More likely the sari was an attempt to disguise her identity, thought de Silva. 'Did she explain why she wanted to rent the house?'

The big man shrugged. 'I don't ask questions.'

'The rent in advance is enough, eh?' De Silva suspected that Ravindra would also have unorthodox ways of removing tenants who turned out to be unsatisfactory.

'I'd like to take a look around it,' he went on. 'I presume you have a key.'

'Now?'

'Yes.'

Ravindra got slowly to his feet and de Silva saw that as well as being broad, he was of above-average height. 'Get on with your work whilst I'm gone,' he said sharply to the man who had let de Silva in.

As they walked in the direction of the rented house, de Silva noticed a few people giving Ravindra nervous looks. He guessed that the landlord had a reputation for being a man it wasn't wise to tangle with. It crossed his mind that if he was about to uncover incriminating evidence, or the house even turned out to be the place where Venetia was being held, it might be advisable to have some backup. 'On second thoughts,' he said, 'I'll bring one of my officers. It will be good experience for him.'

* * *

It took considerably longer to return to the house by way of the police station than it had done to get from there to the bar. De Silva wondered if this Mrs Collins would be back by the time they arrived, but when Ravindra produced a key and opened the door, silence suggested otherwise.

The house's main room led straight off the street. Its flooring was simple beaten earth, and its whitewashed walls were much scuffed. Furniture consisted of two wooden chairs and a small round table. There were bars on a window at the back that overlooked a weed-infested yard surrounded by a high wall.

To the left of the window, a flight of roughly sawn wooden stairs led to the upper floor. Tucked underneath them was a door that led to a small, dark room containing an earth closet, a chipped white sink, and a table on which there was a gas ring, a couple of blackened pans, an assortment of cheap crockery and cutlery, and a few tins and packets of food. De Silva found it hard to imagine anyone preparing an appetising meal there. Whoever this person was, they didn't seem to require comfortable surroundings. A low door gave access to the yard.

The stairs creaked under their feet as he and Prasanna went up them to the first floor. This consisted of one room with a sloping roof. There was a narrow, metal-framed bed heaped with crumpled bedclothes, a small trunk, a chair and perhaps in an attempt to make the place look cosier, a brightly coloured woven rug on the floor.

Prasanna went to the trunk and looked inside. 'There are men's clothes in here, sir.'

He pulled out a pair of trousers and held them up. They were obviously made for a man. 'And this shaving kit.' He held open a black leather pouch to show a good quality shaving brush, and a cutthroat razor.

De Silva thought of the way the "lady" had walked when he'd seen her leaving the house. Even though she had been wearing a sari, her stride had been long, and her pace brisk. He turned to Ravindra. 'I think it's a reasonable assumption that this British lady or yours is a man, don't you?' he asked dryly. 'Carry on searching, Prasanna.'

A truculent expression came over Ravindra's face. 'I didn't know I was being lied to. Whoever it was kept their face covered and spoke very softly.'

'Hmm, I find it hard to believe that you were deceived, but if you co-operate now, I'm prepared to overlook the fact that you've very probably been aiding a fugitive from justice. Exactly what did this person have to say for themselves?'

'As I told you, they paid the rent a month in advance. They were most insistent that if anyone came to me asking for them, I was to deny I knew them, but tell them I'd had a visitor.'

'Did they give a reason?'

'Something about hiding from a cruel husband. They needed time to make arrangements to leave Nuala and go to a safe place.'

'Sir!' Prasanna called from inside an eaves cupboard at the other end of the room. 'I've found something interesting.' He ducked out of the cupboard, brushing cobwebs from his dark hair with one hand and holding in the other a brown manila folder tied with red string. He brought it over to de Silva. De Silva pointed to the brightly coloured rug. 'Lay it there and we'll have a look.'

Prasanna put down the folder and untied the strings. Inside were numerous sketches and watercolours.

'There's more, sir. Shall I bring it all out?'

'Yes.' De Silva began to leaf through the pictures. One of them was the painting of the bazaar he'd seen Tranter doing. Prasanna emerged again from the cupboard with an eager expression on his face. He held a box of watercolour paints and a bundle of artists' brushes.

De Silva smiled. 'Well, I think we've seen everything we need.' He turned to Ravindra. 'You may lock up now, but I'm only accepting your story that you're innocent of any deception on condition that you tell no one about our visit, do you understand?'

Ravindra gave a grudging assent.

De Silva held out his hand. 'I'll keep the key for the moment. And if you hear from this person that they're leaving, you must report it to the police station immediately, is that understood?'

* * *

'I think we can be sure that we've found Laurence Tranter,' said de Silva as he and Prasanna returned to the station. 'The question is, what's he doing living in secret in Nuala? There was no sign of another person being at the house. If Elspeth's right and he's involved with Venetia, she must be hiding elsewhere.'

'I suppose it would be safer for them to keep apart for the moment, sir. Do you think this means that Geraldine Fraser isn't involved?'

'I think it's unlikely. Don't worry about inquiring into her past for the moment. It looks increasingly probable that Elspeth MacDonald has been on the right track.' He smiled ruefully. 'It's a useful if unpalatable lesson, Sergeant, that sometimes in this job one has to eat humble pie, and I expect Elspeth MacDonald will want me to stomach a large slice.'

Prasanna grinned. 'I'll bear that in mind, sir. I'm sorry, I forgot to mention that she's already been on the telephone twice this morning.'

'I thought she might be,' said de Silva gloomily.

'She wasn't happy to hear that you weren't available.'

'Ah well, I'll just have to live with that. Now, if Tranter comes back, I don't want him vanishing off the scene again. I'm afraid you and Nadar had better take turns keeping an eye on the house. It would be best if you can find some way of doing so unobtrusively.'

'That's not a problem, sir. I have some cousins who live in the same street. I'm sure they'll be prepared to help.'

'Excellent.'

The police station came into view, basking in the afternoon sun. De Silva was reminded that he hadn't spoken to Archie and was no further forward with his idea that the abandoned plantation mentioned in the nature notes column in the *Nuala Times* might be the key to finding Venetia. Even if it was too late to enlist Guy Richardson's help and go there today, he could at least approach Archie.

In the public room, Nadar was on the telephone, a perplexed expression on his face. De Silva had a nasty feeling that he knew who was on the other end of the line.

Nadar cupped his hand over the receiver. 'It's Elspeth MacDonald, sir. Shall I say you've arrived?'

'Yes, you'd better.' He might as well get the call over with. 'Oh and bring me some tea, would you?' He would have been glad of something stronger to help him face Elspeth, but police regulations forbade it when one was on duty.

In his office, he waited for the telephone to ring then picked up the receiver.

'At last,' said an irritable voice. 'I hope you have news for me.'

De Silva mastered his irritation. 'Good afternoon, Miss MacDonald, I do indeed. I've established that Laurence

Tranter is still in Nuala. My men are watching the house where he's staying. We're ready to take action as soon as he returns there.'

Elspeth's tone was suspicious. 'Where is this house? I must see it for myself. Where is it?'

'I wouldn't advise you to approach Tranter, ma'am.'

Elspeth snorted. 'I have no desire to do your job for you, Inspector.' He heard the implication in her voice that it was exactly what she wanted, but he was careful not express annoyance. It had been a forlorn hope that the news might take the wind out of her sails. He listened patiently as she expanded on her opinion of his handling of the case to date, and had only just put the receiver down when Nadar came in with his tea.

'I hope the lady is in a better temper now, sir,' he said as he found space for the cup and saucer on de Silva's desk.

'I'd like to think so, but I rather doubt it.' He took a sip of the hot tea, inhaling its soothing fragrance and feeling it calm the churning in his stomach. 'Thank you for this,' he raised the cup. 'When I've finished it, I'll go up to the Residence. I have an idea that someone who works there might be able to help us with finding Venetia MacDonald.'

He explained about the dirty jeep and the place where the moths had been found. He had to admit to himself that the more times he went over the theory, the more tenuous it sounded, but if Nadar thought so too, he didn't let it show. 'Sergeant Prasanna has brought me up to date about the house you want watching, sir,' he said when de Silva had finished. 'He's gone off to take the first shift. I'm to relieve him later tonight.'

'Good. After I've seen Mr Clutterbuck, I'll probably go home. If you want, you may leave early and get yourself something to eat before you take over.'

'Thank you, sir.'

* * *

On the way to the Residence, de Silva realised that he hadn't checked whether Archie would be available to see him. If not, he had to hope that someone at the Residence would be able to point him in the direction of Guy Richardson. He arrived, however, to find that he was in luck. 'The sahib is by the lake,' said the servant who went to enquire if Archie was free when he returned. 'He asks you to join him.'

De Silva wondered if he might find Archie fishing, but he was calling Lady, who was darting about in the tangled vegetation on the bank of the lake. From the look of her damp coat, she had been for a swim. He envied her.

'Dratted dog, she'll get a nasty bite if she isn't careful,' Archie said as de Silva came close. It was clear from the excited wagging and barking that Lady had found something. De Silva looked more closely and saw a monitor lizard. From the top of its dragon-like head to the tip of its tail, it was about four feet long, its scaly body a dull grey with buff markings, supported by muscular, splayed legs. De Silva was aware that although a monitor's venom was unlikely to be harmful to humans, it was dangerous for animals. He wasn't surprised that Archie was concerned.

Fortunately, the arrival of a visitor distracted Lady for a moment. She trotted over to greet de Silva, and he seized the opportunity to grab her by the collar. Archie smiled broadly. 'Well done, you've arrived at the opportune moment. Darcy had the sense to avoid monitors and snakes, but Lady doesn't always have the same instinct for avoiding danger.' He clipped a leash onto her collar. 'She's had plenty of exercise, so we may as well go back to the house, and you can tell me what's been going on.'

The sun was already low, casting long shadows on the grass. Dusk wasn't far off. In Archie's study, the ceiling fan whirred gently. He went to his desk. 'Shut the door, would you, de Silva?' He tapped Lady on the nose. 'And you're staying inside for now.' The Labrador lay down and rested her head on her front paws. Her brown eyes had a look of contrition in them. Archie's expression softened a little as he sank into his chair and gestured to de Silva to take the one opposite.

'Well, what have you got for me? I take it this is about the MacDonalds.'

De Silva nodded and proceeded to explain about Laurence Tranter.

'Quite a stroke of luck,' said Archie when he had finished. He reached out and pulled the brass chain on his desk lamp; the green shade glowed, spreading a pool of light. 'Let's hope Elspeth MacDonald will be pacified for a while. She's called me twice today.' He raised an eyebrow. 'No need to worry, I'm taking her views with a pinch of salt. I'm sure you're doing everything possible.'

'Thank you.'

'So, where do we go next?' asked Archie. 'Any ideas apart from trying to apprehend Tranter?' He listened as de Silva explained his theory about the muddy jeep he'd seen on his visit to Waverley and its connection to the place Guy Richardson had written about. When he came to an end, Archie's silence was discouraging, but then he nodded. 'You've arrived at this one by ingenious, some might say overly ingenious, means, but over the years, I've come to respect your hunches.'

'It's good of you to say so, sir.'

'I think it's worth further investigation. Leave it with me and I'll speak to Guy Richardson. We could go early tomorrow morning, and take him along as our guide, but make sure to let me know if you find Tranter tonight. He may be our man after all.'

'I will.'

'Good. Anything else to tell me before you go?'

'I was thinking that if we find Venetia, it would be useful to have Doctor Hebden with us.'

'Fair point, whatever the situation she may not be in good shape. I'll leave it to you to have a word with him. When I've spoken to Guy, I'll know more about how long it will take us to get to this place. Will you be at home this evening?'

De Silva nodded.

'Then I'll send a message to let you know what time we'll pick you up in the morning. No point getting to the place before it's light, but I'd like to make the search as early as possible. I have an important meeting at lunchtime.'

As de Silva drove home he wondered whether Archie would have been as amenable to the venture, or prepared for such an early start, if Venetia MacDonald had been not quite so attractive.

CHAPTER 11

'It's been a long day,' de Silva said with a yawn when he reached home and found Jane in the drawing room. The ceiling fan hummed, stirring the air and cooling it a little. 'And a hot one,' he added, bending down to stroke the cats who had left the spots where they had been curled up snoozing and come to greet him. Recently, Billy had developed a fondness for the top of the bookcase, and Bella liked to tuck herself behind a copper pot that contained a luxuriant hart's tongue fern.

'Yes, I was at the meeting of one of Florence's committees for the independence celebrations today and everybody was complaining about the heat. It has been exceptionally warm.'

De Silva sighed. 'I'd almost forgotten about the celebrations.'

'But I'm sure you told me that your preparations for the day were well advanced.'

'Well yes, they are, but I'd rather have a clear head and be able to concentrate on them.'

'That's perfectly natural but try not to worry. Why don't you have a wash and put some fresh clothes on? That should make you feel better. I just want a word with cook about dinner then we can sit on the verandah and have a drink.'

'Good idea.'

A short while later, washed and dressed in his coolest

tunic and a pair of loose trousers, de Silva poured himself a whisky and soda and Jane a sherry and took them out to the verandah. He handed Jane her drink and sat down in his chair. Bella, who had followed him, jumped onto his lap and curled herself into a ball. He felt the gentle throb of her purring as he scratched her behind one ear.

'Well, what's kept you so busy today?' asked Jane.

De Silva explained about the cobra and how the incident had led him to the house where he believed Laurence Tranter was staying. 'Prasanna and I found clothes there that would be about the right size for a man of Tranter's build, as well as a shaving kit that included a brush that I believe is of a fairly expensive British make. The most telling thing, however, was the painting equipment that we found. Brushes, paints, and a folder of sketches and watercolours, including the one that I'm sure I saw him working on when I met him at the bazaar. The owner of the house was with us, a fellow called Ravindra who also owns a bar called the Golden Monkey and several properties in town. At first, he claimed that he thought he was letting this one to a lady who was hiding from a cruel husband, but faced with the evidence, he backed down. He's agreed to get in touch if he sees Tranter, and Prasanna and Nadar are taking turns to watch the house.'

'So, one snake led you to another. I do like that,' said Jane. 'But what about Venetia? If Elspeth's right, and she and Tranter are having an affair and conspiring to poison William, might she have also been hiding at the house?'

'Perhaps at one time, but when we searched, we didn't find anything that looked as if it belonged to a woman.'

'I see.'

'Anyway, by the time I got back to the station, Elspeth had been on the telephone several times wanting to know why matters weren't moving more quickly.'

'Was she at all mollified by the news about Tranter?'

'Not noticeably. She pressed me to tell her where this house was, but I held out. I wouldn't put it past her to try and confront him. I don't think that would be at all advisable.'

'Absolutely not. She might endanger herself.'

'And if Elspeth's the one who's abducted Venetia,' said de Silva with a smile, 'it might be Tranter who's in danger.' He took a sip of his whisky. 'If she's using him as a scapegoat, the last thing she'll want is for me to find him. He might have a cast-iron alibi.'

'That's true, although he must have some reason for disguising himself and giving this landlord Ravindra a false name. She paused for a moment. 'On the other hand, if he and Venetia really did conspire to poison William, why stay in Nuala and risk being found? Wouldn't it be safer to leave as soon as possible after it seemed likely that William would recover? I suppose they might not have the means to do so, or think it's safer to lie low, but from what you saw, they aren't hiding together. Doesn't it strike you as odd?'

'Yes, and I don't know the answer to any of it, but with luck, it won't be long before I find out. Will dinner be ready soon?'

Jane laughed. 'You're not too hot to eat, then.'

'Have I ever been?'

'Cook has made a fish curry. I thought that would be nice and light, and we're having watermelon for dessert.'

'Splendid.'

During dinner, de Silva told Jane about his meeting with Archie and the proposed trip in the morning. Like him, she thought Archie's enthusiasm for joining in might have quite a lot to do with a weakness for Venetia. 'Archie's agreed that we should ask David Hebden to come with us,' said de Silva. 'I'll telephone him after dinner.'

Dinner over, de Silva telephoned Hebden who readily agreed, but a few minutes later he rang back. 'Have you changed your mind?' asked de Silva.

'No, but I thought you ought to know that Emerald insists on coming with us. She has a point that if we find Venetia, she might be glad to have the company of another woman, and they are after all, old friends.'

De Silva hesitated. He wasn't at all sure that Archie would be happy with the arrangement, but perhaps his evident soft spot for Venetia would mellow him.

'So are we agreed?' asked Hebden.

'I suppose we are.'

He went back into the drawing room to join Jane. 'Is everything arranged?' she asked.

'Yes.'

Jane looked at him more closely. 'What is it?'

'Emerald. She insists on coming too.'

'Do you think Archie will object?'

'I hope not. He seems very easy going where Venetia MacDonald is concerned.'

The telephone rang again in the hall. 'Ah,' said Jane, 'this will probably be the message from him about tomorrow.'

De Silva got up and hurried to the phone. The man calling introduced himself as Guy Richardson.

'I'm sorry to disturb you at this hour,' he said. 'I've been away from my desk all day and only just heard about the plan for this trip. Firstly, let me say how flattered I am that you read my efforts in the paper, and even more so that you remembered them. But on a more important note, I'm delighted to help. The abandoned plantation I wrote about is roughly a one-and-a-half-hour drive from Nuala. It's called Greenvale and used to be the home of a family called Wyndham. The boss has authorised me to say that we'll pick you up at six o'clock. I should warn you that there aren't many paths, so a lot of the walking may be tricky. Best to bring sturdy footwear. I understand Doctor Hebden may be coming with us.'

'Yes, and his wife Emerald has expressed a wish to join

us as well. She's an old friend of Venetia MacDonald's and very concerned about her.'

There was a pause at the other end of the line. 'Does the boss know?'

'I've only just heard myself.'

'If you like, I'll try and square it with him.'

'I'd be grateful.'

They ended the call, and de Silva returned to Jane.

'Was that the Residence?'

'Yes, it was the chap who's going to guide us, Guy Richardson.'

'Did you mention Emerald?'

'I did, and he kindly offered to speak to Archie about her coming. Now, shall we settle down and enjoy what's left of our evening?'

'Yes. I want to finish my book. It's due back at the library the day after tomorrow, but put on some music if you'd like to.'

'No, I'm happy to be quiet and read as well.'

Jane soon appeared to be engrossed in her book, but this time *Great Expectations* failed to distract de Silva from thoughts of the following morning. Eventually, he closed the book and stood up. 'I think I'll take a turn around the garden. Maybe it will help me to sleep better.'

'Are you worried about tomorrow?'

'A little, I suppose. What if we come back with nothing to show for our expedition? Archie may well take a dim view.'

'But you'll all have the satisfaction of having tried a possibility and ruled it out,' said Jane.

'I suppose that's the best way to look at it.'

'I'm certain it is, dear.'

He left her to her reading and went out to the verandah and down the steps onto the lawn. The night sky was clear, and the full moon gleamed like a silver coin. The temperature was several degrees lower than it had been before dinner and the grass was already damp with dew, accentuating the fragrance of the flowers and shrubs. He heard a rustle and saw the cats disappear into the leathery leaves of a rhododendron bush. When he had planted it, it was no higher than his waist; now it was the size of a small tree.

He wondered if Archie really had much faith in tomorrow's expedition. His own optimism was not as robust as he would have liked it to be. The more he thought about the sad remnants of those insects and butterflies plastered to the jeep, the more he feared they were flimsy pegs on which to hang any hopes. Still, he had weathered Archie's wrath before and if his intuition about his boss's admiration for Venetia was to be believed, he would be more disappointed than angry if they found nothing.

By the time he reached the far end of the garden, his thoughts had drifted to the future. It was strange to think that very soon, he would no longer be answerable to Archie. The relationship they had built over the years would be nothing more than a memory. He would continue to be chief inspector in Nuala, but someone new, perhaps based in Kandy or even Colombo, would take Archie's place, and that someone was likely to be one of his own countrymen.

There was more rustling, and Billy reappeared with Bella in his wake. Miaowing, they weaved around his legs until he bent down to stroke them. 'You think it's time for your milk, do you? Very well, we'll go inside and find Delisha.'

* * *

He and Jane had only just fallen asleep when the sound of the telephone woke him. As he got out of bed, he felt a rush of apprehension. Without stopping to find his dressing gown, he hurried to the hall and picked up the receiver. It was Prasanna's voice on the line.

'I'm sorry if I woke you, sir.'

'No matter. What's happening?'

'Nadar had just arrived to take over from me when we saw someone come back to the house. We think it must be Tranter.'

'Where are you now?'

'At the police station. I've left Nadar keeping watch from the house across the road.'

'Stay where you are. I'll fetch you and we'll go back together. Hopefully we can take Tranter by surprise.'

'Yes, sir.'

'I heard you talking,' said Jane sleepily when he returned to their bedroom to dress. 'Is someone here?'

'No, it was Prasanna on the telephone. He thinks Tranter has returned.' He fumbled to do up the last button on his shirt then sat down on the edge of the bed and pulled on a sock. 'I'm meeting him at the station.'

'Please be careful, dear.'

'Don't worry, I will be.'

* * *

De Silva crossed the street to the house and tried the door handle, but as he had expected, the door didn't budge. It was fortunate he had taken the key from Ravindra. He put it in the lock and turned it, but the door still didn't move. He grimaced. As an extra precaution, Tranter must have bolted the door on the inside.

'Shall I take a look around the back, sir?' whispered Prasanna who had followed him. 'Maybe I can find another way to get in.'

'Very well. Nadar and I will wait here. Come back

and tell us what you find. Be careful. I don't want Tranter spooked.'

Prasanna vanished into the shadows and the sound of his footsteps faded. Several minutes ticked by before he reappeared. There were streaks of brick dust on his clothes and hands.

'I think I can get into the yard at the back of the house. I found some old wooden crates to stand on and had a look over the wall. It's a long drop to the yard but I should be able to manage it. A few of the bricks are missing and that will give me footholds.'

De Silva thought quickly. Prasanna was far younger and more agile than he was. It would be best to leave the job to him. He nodded. 'Let's hope Tranter's asleep upstairs and hasn't thought he needs to lock the back door. If you can get in, we should have a good chance of surprising him.'

Once more Prasanna's footsteps faded, and silence descended. De Silva felt a knot of tension tighten in his stomach. A cloud drifted over the moon, and it grew darker. Something brushed against his foot, and he had to clamp his lips together to stop himself from making any noise. When the moonlight returned, he saw a rat scuttle away with a long curl of something that looked like potato peel in its mouth.

It seemed an eternity before he heard the rasp of bolts being drawn back. The door opened and Prasanna stood there.

De Silva grinned. 'Well done,' he whispered, then recoiled as Prasanna's face contorted and he pitched forward. One hand clutched his shoulder and blood oozed from between his fingers. De Silva didn't have time to pull out his gun before a man erupted from the dark house and leapt over Prasanna's prostrate form. With surprising agility, he delivered a hefty punch right between de Silva's eyes, knocking him backwards, and then shot away down the street.

'Don't worry, sir, I'll catch him,' shouted Nadar.

His breath rattling in his throat and his head muzzy, de Silva managed to straighten up to see his constable pelting after the assailant. He was accompanied by two young men de Silva didn't recognise, but the open door of the lookout house suggested they had run out from there. He took a step forward, intending to follow, but his strength had deserted him. He decided to leave the pursuit to younger men and went to help Prasanna who was slumped in the doorway groaning.

CHAPTER 12

'I thought I told you to be careful,' said Jane when de Silva telephoned her from the hospital at Hatton.

'You did, but our Mr Tranter had other ideas.' De Silva gave his forehead an exploratory pat and winced. It still hurt where Tranter had hit him. 'I feel as if a tree's worth of coconuts landed on me.'

'Oh, Shanti. Has anyone examined you?'

'Yes, one of the doctors here. He told me the blow hasn't caused any serious damage and I'll be right as rain in no time. David Hebden turned up and said much the same but none of them know the pain I'm in,' he grumbled.

'Poor you. And it's a mercy that Prasanna wasn't more seriously injured.'

'Yes, at least we have that to be thankful for. They've stitched up his shoulder and he's not in any danger, but they want to keep an eye on him for a few days, to be sure infection doesn't set in. He'll need time off work.'

'Presumably, you didn't object.'

'Of course not.'

'Have you told Archie what's happened?'

'Yes, I telephoned him from the hospital.' Archie had taken being called so late better than he had expected and also offered to tell Guy Richardson about the delay. 'We agreed it's too soon to understand what bearing it has on the case, but at least we have Tranter now. He's locked up at the station with Nadar watching him, on a charge of attacking a police officer, but I haven't had the chance to question him, and I need a few hours' sleep before I do anything else.'

'Hardly surprising with so much going on. Are you still going to the Wyndhams' plantation?'

'Yes, despite the fact we have to set off later than planned, the trip is still on for today.'

Jane laughed. 'I know Archie's a stickler for punctuality but in the circumstances, I'm sure even he understands. When do you need me to be ready?'

'When do I what?'

'You heard me, dear. If Emerald's coming, I am too. She'll be terribly disappointed if we don't find Venetia and I want to support her. Anyway, do you really think I'd let you go without me after the night you've had? Don't worry about Archie,' she added airily. 'I'll handle him.'

'Are you sure?'

'Absolutely certain.'

'We can't set off until he finishes a lunchtime meeting that he has to attend. If we'd been able to keep to the original plan of leaving at six, he would have stayed for as long as possible before returning to Nuala for it. Unfortunately, it means we may end up having to drive back in the dark.'

'How will you get home after your sleep? Shall I drive down and pick you up?'

'That's a kind thought but Hebden's already offered to take me to where I left the Morris in town. I hope to be back for a late breakfast.'

* * *

When de Silva arrived at Sunnybank, he ate a substantial meal that did duty for breakfast and lunch. At least the blow on the head hadn't taken away his appetite. Jane, who had spoken with Archie and got her way far more easily than she had expected to, left him on the verandah drinking a cup of tea and went to change out of her day dress into something more suited to the expedition on which they were about to embark. Whilst she was gone, a secretary telephoned from the Residence to confirm that Archie would be ready at two o'clock.

Jane returned sporting a pair of beige cotton trousers and a white blouse. The tea that de Silva had just taken a mouthful of went down the wrong way and he spluttered.

'What's the matter?'

De Silva coughed then recovered. 'Nothing. It's just that I've never seen you wear trousers.'

Jane made a face. 'I believe lots of women wore them in the war. When they were working on farms and in factories, for example. Emerald persuaded me to buy a pair a while ago. She said they were so comfortable and practical. Isn't that a good enough reason?'

'Certainly it is, but it will take me time to get used to it.'

Jane laughed. 'I'll admit to you now that I've had them for several months and not plucked up the courage to wear them, but this seemed a suitable occasion.'

De Silva drained the last of his tea. 'Right, if we're to be at the Residence at two o'clock, we'd better be on our way.'

* * *

There was no sign of the brass band, and the Union Jack hung limply from the flagpole. De Silva and Jane went up to the front door and he knocked just as the Hebdens' car arrived. When they got out, to his amusement de Silva noticed that Emerald was also wearing trousers. He wondered if they would encounter Florence, and if so, what her reaction would be.

He didn't have to wait long for his curiosity to be satisfied. There was the purr of another engine and the Residence's stately official Bentley came into view. De Silva glimpsed Florence seated in the back. In the front, a uniformed servant sat next to the chauffeur. When the car drew to a halt, he jumped out and went to open the passenger door. Florence emerged dressed in a pink flowery frock and a broad-brimmed fuchsia pink hat decorated with a bunch of artificial roses. De Silva saw her expression register surprise tinged with disapproval.

'How very modern your outfits are, my dears,' she said to Emerald and Jane. 'Wherever are you going?'

But before they had time to answer, Archie appeared from the house with Lady trotting at his heels. He waved and came over to them. 'Right, we're all here except for Guy Richardson.'

'Archie?' Florence looked at him sternly.

Archie glanced at the chauffeur and servant awaiting instructions, no doubt curious to hear what he would say. 'How was your shopping trip, my dear?' he asked awkwardly.

'Exhausting. It was much too hot in Hatton, and I didn't find any of the things I went for.'

'Oh dear, bad show.'

Florence's eyes narrowed as he nodded to the chauffeur and the servant. 'Put the Bentley in the garage and take the memsahib's parcels into the house.'

The two men got back into the car, and it moved away.

'Archie!' Florence repeated, in a more commanding tone. 'I insist on knowing what's going on.'

Archie looked a little sheepish. 'De Silva has an idea about where Venetia MacDonald might be found. We're going to see if he's on the right track. Why don't you explain, de Silva? My wife knows about Elspeth MacDonald's accusations, but I haven't had time to tell her about the latest developments.'

De Silva proceeded to explain, finishing with the jeep that he'd seen at the Waverley plantation.

'In a roundabout way, it was thanks to Guy Richardson that de Silva made a connection to the plantation that old Giles Wyndham tried and failed to make a go of,' said Archie when de Silva paused. 'Guy mentioned it in that wildlife column he writes for the *Nuala Times*.'

De Silva waited for Florence to pour scorn on his idea but to his relief, her tone changed. 'Do you know, Inspector, shocking as the idea of Elspeth and her brother abducting Venetia is, I think you may have hit on something. And I remember the Wyndhams. It must be twenty years since they gave up their business and went home to England, but before that, they and the MacDonalds were part of the same social circle. Rumour had it that their eldest son might even propose to Elspeth, but in the end, he went back to England with the rest of the family. I've never had a great deal of sympathy for Elspeth. She's always been rather prickly, but I did feel sorry for her then. It must have been a great disappointment when James Wyndham left Nuala. In any case, I believe you can be sure that Elspeth and Douglas know where the plantation is. At one time they were probably regular guests.'

Her remarks allayed a concern that had been troubling de Silva. It was good to know that Elspeth and Douglas would have a reason to choose the Wyndham plantation.

Archie looked at his watch. 'I told Guy two o'clock. Ah, here he is.' He raised a hand and beckoned brusquely to Guy who had just come out of the house. Like his boss and David Hebden he was dressed in a khaki shirt and knee-length shorts with thick woollen socks and sturdy boots. He hurried over to the group, and Lady bounced forward to greet him.

'Sorry, sir, unavoidably detained.'

Archie grunted. 'We're taking the shooting brakes. Best

thing if we encounter obstacles. You go in front with de Silva and Jane, Guy. The rest of us will follow you.'

He reached into his pocket and pulled out a small piece of soft white fabric. When he held it up, de Silva saw it was a lady's glove. 'I sent one of the servants up to Waverley to fetch this. It belongs to Venetia. Her maid confirmed she wore the gloves recently and they haven't been laundered. I thought it might help us to have something with her scent on it. We'll see if Lady can sniff out our quarry. It will be good practice for her.'

* * *

Guy Richardson proved to be a speedy but excellent driver and keen to talk about what was clearly his passion for the flora and fauna of Ceylon, describing numerous off the beaten track expeditions that he had made and the creatures he had seen. He had found out about the possibility of seeing interesting specimens at the Wyndhams' plantation from an old field guide he'd borrowed from the Residence's library.

'We're making good time,' he said as he turned onto a narrower road marked only by an illegible, broken-down sign. 'When I estimated how long the journey would take, I forgot to allow for the fact that it was dark when I drove here on my own. It wasn't easy to see if there were any hazards, so I had to drive more slowly.'

The road narrowed again as high banks, dense with trees and tangled undergrowth, rose up on either side. Today it was dry, but there was evidence of a recent mudslide. De Silva understood why the jeep had been so dirty. Guy slowed down as the shooting brake bumped awkwardly along. 'I'm sorry it's not very comfortable,' he shouted cheerfully over the noise of the protesting engine. 'Not much further to go now.'

They turned a corner, and the bungalow and its outbuildings lay before them. Most of the roofs had fallen in leaving blackened skeletons of beams through which sprouted young trees and other vegetation. At the windows, shutters with flaking green paint hung askew from broken hinges. What was left of the verandah that ran across the front of the bungalow had almost disappeared under a thick tangle of greenery. The steps leading up to it were festooned with luxuriant creepers. De Silva studied the scene with mounting dismay. He hoped there was another entrance. If not, it was impossible to see how anyone could have got into the bungalow.

Guy brought the shooting brake to a halt and Archie drew up alongside. 'Sad to see the place in such a bad state,' he said. 'I'm afraid Wyndham didn't have much of a head for business, and this is the result.'

Emerald looked around her and shivered. 'What an awful place.'

Hebden squeezed her shoulder. 'Don't worry, if Venetia's here, she won't have to put up with it for much longer.'

Archie lifted up the back of the shooting brake and Lady jumped down. 'Good girl,' he said encouragingly and held out Venetia's glove for her to sniff. Tail wagging, she buried her damp, black nose in it then after a moment trotted away, nose now firmly fixed to the ground. Archie beamed. 'She's got the scent. Off we go.'

After a brief exploration around the bottom of the steps leading up to the verandah, Lady continued along the front wall. Where it ended, she raised her head and gave a bark then disappeared around the corner. The group hurried after her. Soon they found themselves at a place where a narrow gap in the undergrowth led to a door. Barking loudly now, Lady pawed at the base of it.

Guy leaned over her and tried the handle. 'It's locked, but the wood looks fairly rotten. I think I can get it open. I've a bag of tools in the shooting brake. I'll fetch it.'

'Stand back everyone,' boomed Archie when Guy returned. 'Give him some room. Lady! Here, girl.' Lady, who had remained at the door wagging her tail and whining, trotted to his side. He put a hand on her collar.

Guy produced a tyre iron from the tool bag and slid it into the gap at the bottom of the door where the wood was rottener than elsewhere. Vigorously, he worked the iron up the gap until he reached the lock then he picked up a hammer. After a series of hefty blows, the lock gave way, and the door opened.

Lady broke free from Archie's grasp and dashed inside barking again. The rest of them followed her through a series of damp, musty rooms that looked as if they had been used for household storage, emerging into a larger, shabby room that appeared to have been part of the servants' quarters. Stains disfigured the walls, and a large portion of the ceiling had collapsed. An electric cable dangled from a beam, and on the ground below it a tarnished copper strip light lay in a twinkling pool of broken glass.

Archie held Lady's collar. 'Steady, girl, we don't want you cutting your paws. Careful where you step, everyone.'

They skirted around the broken glass then Archie released Lady, who rushed to the bottom of a bare wooden staircase and bounded up it. De Silva heard the faint sound of someone calling for help.

'I think we've found her,' said Archie triumphantly.

On the gloomy landing at the top of the stairs, three doors confronted the party. Lady pawed at one of them, barking excitedly.

'This one's locked too,' said Guy. 'But the wood's thin. A few good kicks should get it open.'

Emerald grabbed his arm. 'Please be careful.'

'I will.' He put his mouth to the door. 'Mrs MacDonald? Are you in there? I'm going to break the door down, please keep as far back as you can.'

They waited a moment. De Silva thought he heard a voice say "yes".

'It's Venetia, I'm sure of it,' said Emerald.

Guy aimed a kick and then another. On the fourth attempt, the door gave way.

As de Silva peered into the tiny, ill-lit room, a sour smell rolled towards him. It was insufferably hot. There was an iron bedstead with a dirty mattress and huddled on the floor next to it, Venetia MacDonald. Her dress was torn, and her hair tangled. Emerald gave a gasp of horror and rushed to crouch beside her. 'Venetia, darling. Thank heavens we've found you.'

Shakily, Venetia put her arms around her friend's neck and began to cry. 'I thought it was him coming back again but when I heard barking, I began to hope. I know he doesn't have a dog.'

'Who, darling?'

'Douglas, William's brother. He brought me here.'

Hebden put a hand on his wife's shoulder. 'Let me examine her, Emerald. There'll be plenty of time for questions later.'

'Come and stand with me, Emerald,' said Jane, reaching out a hand.

Hebden knelt down beside Venetia. 'You're safe now. We'll soon have you out of here.' He felt her pulse. There were sores on her wrists. 'Were you tied up?'

'Yes, for a while.'

'I have some antiseptic that will deal with these sores but what you need most is fluid. Do you remember when you last had any food or water?'

'He came back to bring me some, but I'm not sure when. So little light comes through the window that it's been hard to know whether it's day or night.'

'Let's get you out into the fresh air. Do you think you can walk?'

'I'll try.'

Hebden stood up and helped her to her feet. 'Here, put your arm around my shoulder. Guy, you take the other side.' Between them they helped Venetia to the landing but there she slumped. 'I'm sorry, I can't go any further,' she said, her eyes closing.

'I'll find something we can use as a stretcher,' said Guy. 'I think there's a tarpaulin in the shooting brake.'

'Good man,' said Archie.

Guy was soon back with the tarpaulin. 'I've brought along a canteen of water too,' he said.

'Well done,' said Hebden. 'Bathing her face should cool her down and we may be able to get her to drink a little.'

Between them, he and Guy laid out the tarpaulin and gently lifted Venetia onto it. Emerald produced a handkerchief and dabbed some of the water from the canteen on Venetia's face but only succeeded in moistening her friend's lips.

Carefully, Guy and Hebden lifted the ends of the canvas and manoeuvred it down the stairs. The others watched them go.

Emerald wiped away a tear. 'How could anyone be so cruel? Douglas must be a monster to do something like this.'

Archie gave a grunt of acquiescence. 'Don't worry, my dear, we'll find him, and he'll pay for it.'

He took de Silva aside. 'It's a shocking state of affairs. Do you think he acted on his own or do you still believe Elspeth's guilty too?'

'I do, sir.'

'Hmm, you're probably right. I've always had the impression Douglas was under her thumb and doesn't have much backbone. It's lucky the situation isn't any worse. If something had happened to prevent Douglas coming out here, the consequences might have been disastrous. I'm curious as to why she was being kept alive, but as, thank goodness, she's safe now, we should soon know the whole story. We'd better make sure that she's admitted to hospital discreetly. We don't want Elspeth and Douglas knowing just yet that she's been found.'

Guy reappeared. 'We're ready to go, sir, but with Mrs MacDonald on board, I'm afraid there will only be room for the driver and another person in one of the shooting brakes.'

Archie raised an eyebrow. 'I think that's the least of our problems, don't you?'

'What if Douglas comes back and realises that Venetia's been rescued before Shanti has a chance to arrest him?' asked Jane.

'A very good point,' said Archie. 'Any ideas?'

'I'll stay here and watch for him, sir,' said Guy. 'I've a hunting rifle in the shooting brake. I'll keep it with me.'

'Excellent. Hebden or de Silva can drive back to Nuala in your place. I'll send out another vehicle and a couple of chaps to give you any help you need.'

* * *

De Silva offered to drive and went ahead with Jane and Emerald. They had made Venetia as comfortable as possible on the rear seat of the other vehicle which Archie drove, with Hebden doing his best to keep an eye on her.

As de Silva predicted, darkness had fallen, so he drove more slowly than he was accustomed to doing. It wasn't long, however, before he lost sight of Archie who, with Venetia on board, must be taking the road even more cautiously. The shooting brake's headlights illuminated the way ahead with their yellowish light, but on either side of the road the countryside was shrouded in darkness. He had just rounded a bend when a strange-looking cloud that hung about five feet above the road appeared a little way in front of him. He slowed, hoping that if Archie caught up, he would notice the brake lights and follow suit.

'What's wrong?' asked Jane. 'Why are you stopping?'

'There's something up ahead.'

'It's moving,' said Emerald after a moment. 'It looks as if it's a big bundle of dried leaves or scraps of paper.'

Suddenly, the cloud fragmented, and de Silva realised that it wasn't made up of leaves or paper scraps, but of dozens of Atlas moths. As they were caught in the headlights, he marvelled at their huge size and beautiful chestnut, white, and ochre markings, then they rose like a cresting wave, flew over the shooting brake's roof and disappeared into the darkness of the trees to one side of the road.

'Gracious, what a marvellous sight,' said Jane. 'And what a pity that nice young man Guy wasn't here to see it.'

'Marvellous indeed,' said de Silva as a stray Atlas moth fluttered on by, 'but I expect he'll have other chances.'

'Anyway,' Jane went on. 'What we found tonight matters more than anything.'

They had almost reached the outskirts of Hatton when de Silva heard hooting. Looking in his rear mirror, he saw that Archie was now not far behind with his arm out of the window flagging them down. De Silva stopped and waited whilst Hebden got out and came over to them.

'I know a quiet entrance into the hospital. Let us go ahead and you can follow us.'

'Very well. How's Venetia doing?'

'She's been asleep most of the way. Best thing for her at the moment. Once we get her to hospital, I'm fairly confident it shouldn't be too long before she recovers. Archie thinks that in the interest of not drawing attention to what's going on, it's best that we alert the hospital that we need a room, then I'll go in alone with Venetia and take her straight to it. Archie will drive the rest of you back to Nuala.'

* * *

Archie drove Emerald and the de Silvas to Sunnybank, where Emerald accepted Jane's invitation to stay until there was more news of Venetia. Afterwards de Silva and Archie went on to the Residence. They were met in the reception hall by Florence. Fortunately, as work was over for the day, there was no one else about.

'What's happened?' she asked. 'Did you find her?'

Archie drew her aside. 'Yes, but we'll go to my study before I tell you about it. The last thing we want is any of this getting out before de Silva's ready to make an arrest.'

Florence looked shocked. 'Oh my goodness—'

Archie put a finger to his lips. 'Wait until we're in my study.'

For once, Florence didn't argue. Archie stood aside to let her go first, then with Lady trotting at their heels, he and de Silva followed. Briefly, he thought how strange it still seemed to see Florence without her little dog Angel. He had died a short while after Archie's old Labrador Darcy.

'De Silva is to be congratulated,' said Archie once they were in the study with the door closed behind them. 'He was on the right track. We found Venetia tied up at the Wyndhams' old place. She was in poor shape, but she's in hospital now and Hebden's confident she'll soon be on the mend.'

Florence's brow furrowed. 'Has she told you what happened to her?'

'Yes, it was Douglas who took her to the plantation, but it's not clear yet what part Elspeth had in the kidnapping. Venetia needs some rest before she tells us the whole story.'

Florence sat down heavily on one of the mahogany chairs. 'Poor child,' she said sadly. Lady, who had taken up her usual place beside her master's chair, raised her head and whimpered. Archie bent down and put a hand on her glossy black head.

'It's shocking that anyone would do something like this,' Florence went on. 'Especially to one of their own family. So, what are you going to do?'

Archie and de Silva exchanged glances. Archie spoke first. 'I'm prepared to leave the decision to you, de Silva, but in my view, it's best to wait until Venetia's able to tell us exactly what happened. We've a good case against Douglas, but if Elspeth denies any involvement, she won't be an easy woman to crack. We'll need to have our facts straight. Hopefully, we won't have to wait long. In the meantime, the news that Venetia's been found must be kept under wraps. I don't want to risk it getting out. At the moment, I think we can presume that Elspeth and Douglas don't know we've found her, and whilst that's the case, I don't think there's any danger of them trying to get away, but in any case, before you go, de Silva, I suggest we give Hebden a call at the hospital and find out how matters are progressing.'

* * *

When he arrived home, Billy and Bella emerged from the pool of shade Jane's car cast on the driveway and came over to greet him, purring like little dynamos as he stroked their sleek, dark fur. He felt heat radiate from their bodies and shuddered at the memory of how Venetia MacDonald must have suffered and the fear she must have felt. As Archie had observed, if something had prevented Douglas from bringing Venetia food and drink, the situation might have been so much worse. He thought of the clues that had led them to finding her. They reinforced his belief that one must never dismiss anything, no matter how remote the chance of it leading to a solution.

'Shanti, aren't you coming in?' Jane stood on the front doorstep in the glow of the porch light.

'I'm sorry, I was far away.'

She came over to kiss his cheek. 'I know, it's a horrible thing to have happened. And if it distresses us to think about what Venetia must have suffered, it's much worse for Emerald. I manage to persuade her to try to rest in the spare room. I crept up just before I heard your car and she's sleeping, thank goodness. Do you know what's happening at the hospital?'

'Yes, Archie telephoned David Hebden. He said that Bradley-Clarke has examined Venetia and confirms that she should soon be right as rain. He wants to keep her under observation, but doubts she'll suffer any lasting effects.'

'Thank goodness for that. I'm glad we have some good news for Emerald when she wakes up.'

CHAPTER 13

Later that night, Hebden returned from Hatton to collect Emerald and drive her home, so de Silva and Jane were alone at breakfast the following morning when he called with more news from the hospital.

'Bradley-Clarke has just telephoned me to say that he's happy for Venetia to answer any questions you have.'

'Have they managed to keep it secret she's there?'

'Bradley-Clarke assures me that no one but he and a few of the nurses are aware of it.'

'Good. I'll go down straight away. Thank you for letting me know.'

'I can tell from your expression that it's good news,' said Jane as he sat down again at the dining room table.

'Indeed it is, Venetia's well enough to answer questions.' He picked up his fork and speared a piece of omelette. 'I think I can afford a moment or two to finish this off, then I'll be on my way.'

On the drive to the hospital, he decided that a wise precaution would be to go to William MacDonald's room before he spoke to Venetia. Presumably, Elspeth was still with him and if it somehow slipped out that he had been seen at the hospital, he wanted her to believe that a visit to William was his reason for coming. If it meant enduring another scathing attack on his competence, it was a small price to pay.

At the hospital, he went to the reception desk and spoke to an efficient-looking lady who confirmed that William was still in the same room and Elspeth was with him. Gloomily, de Silva went to find them.

William's room was cool and dimly lit. The curtains at the tall window were drawn half closed and billowed gently in the current of air stirred up by the ceiling fan. Elspeth sat in an armchair in the corner of the room. She put down the piece of sewing she was working on and regarded de Silva balefully.

'Is my sister-in-law still missing?' she asked sharply. 'How much longer is this going to take?'

De Silva forced himself to be polite. It was tempting to tell Elspeth the truth and call her bluff, but he must restrain himself until he'd spoken to Venetia. 'I hope to have news for you soon, ma'am.'

He studied Elspeth's expression. If she had any qualms about what that news would be, she didn't let them show. She gestured to the bed where William lay. 'You can see for yourself what a terrible thing she's done to my poor brother. She poisoned him, I'm sure of it, and that man Tranter helped her.' Her lips compressed into a grim line.

Despite himself, de Silva felt a niggle of uncertainty. If Elspeth was guilty, she was putting on a good show, but he couldn't dismiss quite yet the possibility that Douglas had acted alone and she was an innocent party. If that was the case, although her behaviour was galling, it was forgivable.

'Have you spoken with Doctor Bradley-Clarke this morning?' he asked.

Elspeth nodded. 'He says William's heartbeat is steadier, but he's still unable to tell me if...' her voice faltered, 'if he'll be entirely well when he regains consciousness.'

De Silva felt a twinge of pity for her. Elspeth might well have committed a heinous crime, but he felt sure that her devotion to her brother was genuine.

* * *

After he left William and Elspeth, de Silva returned to the reception desk and quietly asked for someone to show him to Venetia's room. The receptionist made a telephone call and after a few moments, a nurse arrived to take him there.

'I'll come in with you and make sure Mrs MacDonald's comfortable then leave you to have your conversation,' she said. 'But if she shows any signs of distress, please call me in straight away.'

Venetia was dozing when they entered the room. The nurse went over to her and put a hand on her shoulder.

'Mrs MacDonald, dear, you have a visitor.'

Venetia opened her eyes. For a moment she looked blank then she smiled. 'Inspector de Silva, I'm so glad to see you.'

Her face was bare of makeup, and she looked wan, but a spark of the vitality that had charmed de Silva when he had first seen her still remained.

The nurse helped her to sit up, then plumped her pillows and straightened the bedsheet with a practised hand. 'There, how's that? Are you comfortable?'

'Very, thank you.'

'The Inspector wants to ask you a few questions, but he understands that he mustn't tire you. I'd like you to drink some water before he starts.'

There was a carafe of water and a glass on the bedside table. The nurse poured some of the water into the glass and gave it to Venetia who took a few sips before handing it back.

'Well done,' the nurse said in an encouraging tone. She put the glass on the bedside table and moved the call bell that dangled from one side of the bedhead to within Venetia's reach. 'If there's anything you want, press the button and I'll come straight away.' She nodded to de Silva. 'I'll be just outside.'

'I believe I have you to thank for finding me,' said Venetia when the door closed.

'I can't claim all the credit.'

'I'm sure you ought to claim the major part, and I'm extremely grateful. Now, what would you like to ask me?'

De Silva extracted his notebook and a pen from his jacket pocket. 'I hope you have no objection to my writing down what you have to say.'

'Of course not.'

'Then shall we begin? When we found you, you told us that it was your brother-in-law Douglas who kidnapped you.'

'Yes.'

'Was your sister-in-law involved?'

'She was, I'm not sure that Douglas would have done anything on his own. I suspect she put him up to it. She's by far the stronger character of the two. I was all too aware that she's never liked me. I suppose that in her eyes I was an interloper who stood between her and William. The three of them were quite young when their parents died and, with no other family in Ceylon, only had each other for support. I'm sure Elspeth would have preferred that to remain the case. William said from the start that given time, she would come round, and we'd become friends. I didn't like to be discouraging, but I wasn't optimistic.'

Her slim fingers bunched up the turnover of the bed-sheet, destroying the nurse's neat handiwork; there was a catch in her voice. 'It seems that William and I both underestimated exactly how much she hated me.'

She tried to sit up and reach for the glass of water on the bedside table but failed. De Silva picked it up and gave it to her, then waited whilst she took a few sips.

'I'm sorry.' She handed him back the glass. 'How foolish of me to get emotional when thanks to you, I'm safe. I ought to tell you exactly what happened. That's what you need to know, isn't it?'

'If it's too painful, we can delay our talk for a little longer.'

Venetia shook her head. 'There's no need. I'd rather tell you now. It was nearly five o'clock when I came back to the plantation that day to find that William had been taken ill. Pamu said it had happened very suddenly. As no one else in the family was at home, he'd called for Doctor Hebden who had already sent an ambulance. Elspeth arrived home at about the same time I did, although Douglas was still out when we left for the hospital.'

'Pamu told me that no one knew where William had been that day. Did that include you?'

'Yes. He wasn't expected home for lunch. At breakfast he'd said that he would probably send a message to the kitchen to have something brought down to the factory if he wanted it. I didn't think anything of that. If he was busy, he was quite often away until evening.'

'But I take it he didn't send for his lunch?'

'No, so Pamu assumed he'd made some last-minute arrangement. Perhaps lunching at one of his clubs or the Crown Hotel, maybe with a friend or a business contact.'

'I've already checked with the clubs and the Crown. Your husband didn't visit any of them that day.'

'I'm afraid I wasn't a great deal of help. It was such a shock to see poor William in the state he was in. To her credit, Elspeth took charge and between her and Doctor Hebden they dealt with everything. To be honest, she was far more capable than I would have been. When she was a young woman, she trained as a nurse, but she gave it up when she came back to live at the plantation to keep house for her father.'

'When the two of you reached the hospital, did you think there was anything odd in Elspeth's manner?'

'She was very anxious about William's condition, as was I, but it was no more than one would expect of a sister who loved her brother. Why do you ask?'

'Because I believe it may already have been in her mind to accuse you of trying to poison him.'

Venetia's eyes widened. 'How horrible! But anyway, who would believe anyone wanted to poison William? I can't think of anyone who would want to harm him. Doctor Bradley-Clarke said it was a heart attack.'

'Your husband might have ingested something accidentally, but whatever the case, I'm afraid Elspeth subsequently made that claim.'

Venetia's face was very pale. She had closed her eyes. De Silva feared he had gone too far and wondered if he should let her rest for a while, but then she opened them again and continued. 'As you know, we were at the hospital for hours.' She shivered. 'It was terrible waiting, not knowing whether there was any hope. When the doctor said the immediate crisis was over and suggested we go home and try to get some rest, I still didn't want to leave William. I was quite surprised that Elspeth was so adamant it would be a good idea. I suppose you may be right she was already planning to kidnap me and accuse me of poisoning William. It would be the perfect revenge for what she saw as my crime of taking him away from her, and the perfect way of ridding herself of me for ever.' Her voice rose. 'Has she thought of any other ways of blackening my character?'

De Silva hesitated. It was probably a bad time to mention Tranter.

There was a tap at the door and the nurse put her head around it. 'Is everything alright?' She walked over to the bed and felt Venetia's pulse then looked back at de Silva. 'She needs a few minutes' rest. Please be so kind as to go into the corridor, Inspector. I'll be a moment then I'll show you somewhere you can wait.'

Reluctantly, de Silva got up and left the room. Several minutes later, the nurse reappeared and showed him to an area where there were a few chairs.

'Is there somewhere more private?' he asked.

'Only the main reception area.'

That was likely to be worse. He told her he would stay where he was and sat down gingerly, hoping not too many people would come by and notice him.

During the next half hour, a few porters and nurses passed but only one of them stopped to ask if he needed help. Eventually, the nurse returned and took him back to Venetia's room. She had regained her self-possession, and apologised for the delay.

'There's no need to apologise, ma'am. Are you sure you're ready to talk again?'

She nodded. 'It was almost midnight when we got back to Waverley. Elspeth was actually being very kind to me. She insisted on my having a mug of cocoa and going straight to bed.'

'Who prepared the cocoa?'

'I'm not sure. I imagine it was our cook, although Elspeth brought it up to my room. She told me I wasn't to worry. I could leave her to take care of anything that needed doing. We agreed that we'd come back to the hospital first thing in the morning, but she promised to call me if there was any news before then.'

'This drink of cocoa, did it taste unusual in any way?'

Venetia frowned. 'Do you think she put something in it?'

'It's a possibility. She may have wanted to make you drowsy.'

'Yes, I see that, but if she did, I was so preoccupied with my fears for William, that I'm afraid I didn't notice. I thought I'd never be able to sleep, but in fact I slept almost as soon as my head touched the pillow. I woke to find a figure standing over me. I'd forgotten to draw the curtains and there was moonlight coming through the window. I thought it would be Elspeth bringing me news of William, so although I still felt very sleepy, I tried to sit up. That was when I realised it wasn't her.'

De Silva hesitated. He mustn't put words into her mouth.

'It was a man, but I didn't realise it was Douglas until I heard his voice. Elspeth told him to hurry, and he said something about doing it herself if she didn't trust him. He pushed me back down on the bed and clamped something over my face. I tried to push him away, but I still felt so sleepy and confused. I remember a horrible sickly smell and then everything went black.'

De Silva recalled the chloroform in Angus MacDonald's study. It would have been easy for Elspeth or Douglas to get hold of it.

'When I came round, my hands were tied, and I was gagged and stretched out on the back seat of a moving vehicle. It was very dark, but I guessed it was one of the jeeps from the plantation. William sometimes drove the two of us about in them. I think it was raining heavily. We were sliding around all over the place. Eventually we stopped and it was Douglas who came to get me out.'

'Did he say anything to you?'

'He was oddly polite, helping me out of the jeep very solicitously. The rain hadn't stopped, and he put a water-proof coat over me, but he didn't untie my hands or remove the gag. I was still so groggy that I didn't have the strength to resist him. I don't remember much about how we went inside the bungalow or up to the room.'

'What did he do then?'

'He took off the gag then untied my hands and told me he'd have to leave me there for a while, but he'd take me to somewhere nicer as soon as the time was right. I begged him to let me go but he said he couldn't because of Elspeth. He told me he didn't want to hurt me, but she wanted me dead. She must never find out I was still alive.' She flushed and looked away. 'Then he tried to kiss me. I managed to push him off, but he said he was sure I'd learn to love him in the end. I was so angry. I told him that would never happen. I love William and I always will.'

She stopped, and de Silva saw that she was shaking. He put a hand on her arm. 'Would you rather rest again?'

Venetia shook her head. 'I don't need to, thank you. There isn't much more to tell. Douglas looked sad and said he'd leave me to think about everything and come back. He went out and I heard him lock the door. As I told you, he returned to bring me food and water, but no matter how hard I begged, he still refused to let me go. What will happen now, Inspector? Even if neither of them harmed William, Elspeth had every intention of harming me, didn't she?'

She gulped and knuckled tears from her eyes. 'Poor William, he cares very much for Elspeth, you know, and although he and Douglas haven't always got on well, they are brothers. I can't bear to think of how unhappy all this will make him.'

'I'm afraid they must take the consequences of their crime, ma'am.'

There was a soft tap at the door and the nurse's head appeared around it again. 'Doctor Hebden's here. Shall I show him in?'

Venetia looked at de Silva. 'Do you have any more questions, Inspector?'

'Not at the moment. I'll leave you in Doctor Hebden's capable hands.'

Outside, he met Hebden in the corridor. 'How did it go?' he asked.

De Silva lowered his voice so that the nurse who waited at the door to Venetia's room wouldn't overhear. 'Venetia's confirmed it was Elspeth and Douglas who kidnapped her. They used chloroform to overpower her, very likely taken from Angus MacDonald's study, but Elspeth may already have given her a sedative in a mug of cocoa. Elspeth wanted her dead and presumably still doesn't know that Douglas kept her alive. He's clearly obsessed with her.'

Hebden let out a low whistle. 'So the cat's among the pigeons, eh?' he said quietly. 'This is going to cause a scandal if it gets out and no mistake. What are you going to do now?'

'Arrest them both as soon as possible, but I'd far rather not arrest Elspeth when she's with William.'

'Yes, Bradley-Clarke has been reducing the amount of sedative William's being given, and he may have reached some level of consciousness. It's not a time to administer a shock. Not that it ever will be the right time for one like this.' He scratched his chin. 'Would it help if I removed Elspeth from his room? I could say that I needed a private word and was concerned we might disturb him.'

'Thank you, that would help.'

Hebden nodded to the nurse who was still waiting at Venetia's door. 'I'll be a few moments, nurse. I need to assist Inspector de Silva with something.'

'Very well, doctor. I'll stay here, shall I?'

'Yes, please.'

De Silva followed Hebden along the corridors that led to William's room and waited outside whilst he went in. De Silva heard the murmur of voices; he took a deep breath, readying himself to face Elspeth, then as Hebden emerged from the room with a grim expression on his face, a feeling of foreboding crept up on him. Over his shoulder, de Silva saw a nurse in the room, but there was no sign of Elspeth.

'Bad news, I'm afraid,' said Hebden. 'Elspeth left a short while ago.'

'Did she say anything about where she was going?' de Silva asked the nurse who had followed him out of the room.

She gave him a look of prim disapproval. 'No, and I didn't think it was my place to ask.'

But it was exactly the kind of thing he wanted to know, de Silva thought angrily. He was painfully aware that he was at fault too. Elspeth's apparent devotion had lulled him into a sense of false security. He should have arranged for someone to watch her comings and goings. Still, there was no point dwelling on past mistakes. He needed to concentrate on finding her. He dismissed the nurse and hurried to the hospital reception desk.

'Did anyone see Miss MacDonald leave?'

'Yes,' answered the younger of the two receptionists.

'Did she say where she was going or when she'd be back?'

The young woman shook her head. 'No, and it's rare for her to go out. She usually has fresh clothes and anything else she needs sent in.'

De Silva thanked her and hurried out to the car park. There were a few cars parked there but no one around who might have seen Elspeth and remembered in which direction she went. Unless he was lucky and she'd gone to Waverley, he was going to be looking for a needle in a haystack.

He decided to trust to luck and try Waverley first. Although the hospital receptionist said that anything she needed was usually sent in, he supposed it was possible there was something she had to attend to in person, so this could be an innocent errand. The alternative reason for going back home was that she had realised that the game was up and was bent on escaping, and there were things she didn't want to leave behind. She would also need to warn Douglas that they were in danger. He wondered how many people had known Venetia was also at the hospital. Had it got back to Elspeth? Or had it been his own presence, even though he'd done his best to be unobtrusive?

Fortunately, there was very little traffic about and he was soon able to speed up. When he reached Waverley, he paused for a moment at the fork in the road, then decided to follow the route to the house. It was the right decision. A few moments later, he noticed an approaching car ahead of him. As the gap closed between it and the Morris, he saw that Elspeth was in driver's seat.

He deftly spun the steering wheel to the right and brought the Morris to a halt at an angle that would prevent her from passing him. She braked and slammed her hand on the horn. When he didn't move out of her way, she pulled off the road and tried to drive around the Morris, but her low-slung car soon became stuck.

De Silva jumped out of the Morris and hurried over to her, but she ignored him as she revved the engine in a desperate attempt to drive on. He reached through the window for the ignition key and with a swift twist, pulled it out. The engine spluttered and died.

Elspeth turned on him, her face a mask of fury; she threw open the driver's door, slamming it into him. He fell back winded as she pushed past him and ran for the Morris. With dismay, he realised he had left his own key in the ignition. The next moment she was at the wheel, turning the car to face in the direction from which de Silva had come then shooting away.

He ran after her, but it was no use. His breath came in ragged gasps, and it felt as if his lungs were on fire. He had no chance of catching up with her before she turned onto the main road. Then he saw one of the plantation's trucks coming around the bend a little way ahead. It was in the middle of the road, and he knew that for once, fortune had blessed him. In a desperate attempt to pass the truck without slackening her speed, Elspeth swerved. The screech of brakes and the sickening sound of metal scraping on metal rang in his ears. The Morris came to a halt, and with a tremendous effort, he put on a final burst of speed, reaching it before Elspeth had time to extricate herself. He stumbled forward, yanked the driver's door open, and through the buzzing in his head and the thumping of his heart, heard himself say, "Elspeth MacDonald, you're under arrest.'

CHAPTER 14

Fortunately, the damage to the Morris was not too serious and de Silva was still able to drive her, but by the time he arrived home several hours later, he was exhausted. He found Jane in the garden beside the pond that their gardener, Anif, had created for them the previous autumn. Bella was tucked under her arm, her legs dangling elegantly down Jane's hip. At the sight of de Silva, she squirmed to be free. Jane set her down and she scooted over to greet him.

He bent to stroke her. 'Hello, little one. Are you on your own?'

'No, Billy's here.' Jane pointed to Billy who was prowling around the edge of the pond. 'There's a frog under one of the lily leaves. He's not bold enough to go in to catch it, but I think he hasn't given up hope it will come out of its own accord.'

She looked at him more closely. 'You look thoroughly worn out, dear. What's happened? Has something gone wrong?'

'It very nearly did.'

He told her about Elspeth's flight and subsequent arrest.

'I think she may have overheard some of the nurses talking about Venetia being found. If that's right, as the blunder didn't ruin everything, I don't propose to conduct a witch hunt. I'm afraid the Morris didn't come off unscathed when Elspeth met that truck. There's a nasty dent in the wing and some damage to her paintwork that I'll have to get Gopallawa to deal with.'

'Never mind, you can borrow my car for a few days if you need to.'

'I might take you up on that.'

'Have you found Douglas?'

'We had a stroke of luck there. He came to the Wyndhams' bungalow to bring more food and water to Venetia and ran straight into Guy Richardson. He and the servants that Archie sent up from the Residence to help him brought Douglas to the station where Nadar formally arrested him and locked him up.'

'What about William?'

'Hebden sent a message to the police station that he's regained consciousness.'

'Oh, that's marvellous news. Are he and Venetia together?'

'I'm sure they will be by now. The only fly in the soup is that, if he hasn't heard already, William will have to be told about Elspeth and Douglas.'

'It's ointment, dear. The poor man, how distressing for him.'

Billy stopped prowling along the edge of the pond and put an exploratory paw on a waterlily leaf. He recoiled with a stricken yowl when it sank under the water, and he was almost catapulted in after it.

Jane looked at him sternly. 'That will teach you.' She scooped him up. 'You say Douglas is at the police station but what about Elspeth?'

'She's at the Residence. Archie and I agreed that a cell at the station wasn't appropriate. The Residence isn't ideal with so much going on but he's seeing to it that she's properly accommodated and guarded.'

'Have you eaten?'

'No. Food would be very welcome, and I'll tell you what Venetia had to say.'

* * *

'Poor Venetia, what a dreadful time she's had,' said Jane as she sat with him in the dining room drinking tea whilst he ate.

'Yes, it was clearly hard for her to talk about it,' said de Silva, breaking off a piece of naan to wipe up his curry sauce. 'I admired her determination to do so, and thanks to the story she had to tell, I think we have finally arrived at the solution to the case. Elspeth wanted her brother to herself, and she didn't want the plantation taken away from her. No doubt Douglas was loath to lose his inheritance too, but Venetia doubts he would have acted on his own and believes that Elspeth put him up to kidnapping her. The poor lady was shocked when I told her Elspeth had accused her of poisoning William.'

De Silva popped the morsel of naan into his mouth and swallowed it before he continued. 'So, Elspeth persuaded Douglas to take advantage of William's dramatic collapse to abduct Venetia and claim she had poisoned him in order to inherit his money. Elspeth wanted Douglas to murder Venetia to make sure she never escaped, but what she didn't foresee was that Douglas wasn't prepared to do that. He seems to have been obsessed with Venetia and determined to keep her for himself.'

He ate another piece of naan. 'Maybe Douglas loved her from the beginning and was jealous of William's success with her all this time. He's probably gone through life feeling he's the also-ran, and Elspeth's plan gave him the opportunity he needed to change that and allowed him a chance to have Venetia all to himself, however deluded he may have been.'

'That's very profound, dear.' Jane smiled. 'Anyway, thank goodness he's been thwarted. One dreads to imagine what kind of life poor Venetia would have been condemned to if she hadn't been rescued.'

'Quite.'

'It's a chilling thought that if he eventually gave up hope of winning her over, he might even have killed her as Elspeth wanted him to do in the first place.'

'Indeed it is a chilling thought.'

De Silva mopped up the remains of the curry sauce on his plate. 'I suppose I'd better get back to the hospital. I've been so busy with Elspeth and Douglas that I've yet to find out from William where he was on the day that he collapsed.'

'Must you? You've already had a long day.'

'Yes, my dear, I am a little tired, but duty calls.'

'What about Laurence Tranter?'

'Hmm, I'd almost forgotten about him now that he doesn't seem to have anything to do with the MacDonald case. Yes, it would be interesting to know what he was up to.'

* * *

It was dark by the time he reached the hospital. The bustle of the day over, the reception area was quiet. De Silva gave his name to the receptionist and set off down the corridor that led to William MacDonald's room. Before he had a chance to knock on the door, it opened and a different nurse to the prim one he had encountered on his last visit emerged. She gave him a friendly smile. 'Good evening, Inspector. Mr and Mrs MacDonald are still doing well, but you won't tire them, will you?'

'I'll try my best not to.'

Inside the room, de Silva found William sitting up in bed. His face looked gaunt, but he was clean-shaven and obviously in command of his faculties again. Venetia sat at his bedside. Dressed in a summer frock with her hair neatly arranged and a little makeup on, if she hadn't looked anxious, one wouldn't have guessed that she had suffered such a terrible ordeal. De Silva wondered how much William already knew about Elspeth and Douglas's treachery. This conversation might not be easy.

He took a deep breath. 'First, may I say what a pleasure it is to see you recovered, Mr MacDonald.'

William brushed the pleasantry aside with a brusque nod. 'I would have preferred my recovery not to be greeted by the news about my brother and sister. I'm utterly appalled by what they did. I hope you have them under lock and key.'

Venetia stroked his hand. 'Try not to get agitated, darling. You know it's not good for you, and there's no need. I'm safe now.'

William raised her hand to his lips and kissed it. 'You're very kind-hearted, my love, but there's every reason to be angry. It they'd succeeded in carrying out their plan, matters would have been very different. They must both pay for what they've done.'

'We have them under arrest, sir,' said de Silva. 'You can rest assured that they won't go unpunished.'

William looked sad. 'Foolishly, I feel regret as well as anger. Elspeth and I were very close and although Douglas and I never had the same bond, blood, as they say, is thicker than water.' A muscle twitched in his cheek and de Silva thought he detected moisture in his eyes before he pulled himself together and continued. 'But I digress. I expect you have questions for me, Inspector.'

'Do you really feel up to this now, darling?' asked Venetia. 'I'm sure the Inspector would understand if you don't and would rather wait. Or he could talk to Doctor Hebden, and he could explain what you've already told him.'

'No need for that. I'm sure the Inspector prefers to hear things first hand. Take a seat, Inspector, and fire away.'

De Silva sat down and took out his notebook. 'Thank

you, sir. Shall we start with the morning of the day you collapsed? Your secretary, Geraldine Fraser, mentioned that you visited your office, but left before lunch. Can you recall where you went?'

'Into town. I had some business I wanted to see the bank manager about. I hadn't arranged an appointment, but he made time to meet me.'

Of course he did, thought de Silva. No doubt William was an important client.

'I'd planned to return home for lunch, but whilst I was at the bank, I met a fellow called Cyril Bradshaw. Bradshaw's rather a bore, and not a man I'd ordinarily want to spend time with, but on occasion we've discussed prospective business ventures together. He had a new one he wanted to talk to me about that sounded interesting. I decided to find out more and when he suggested I join him for lunch, I agreed.'

'Where did you have lunch?'

'We went back to his house. He was most insistent about it. Said his wife Helena would be charmed to see me.' The name rang a bell in de Silva's mind. Helena Bradshaw had been the lady at the flower show. 'Their cook had managed to get hold of a joint of beef,' William was saying, 'imported from Australia, and it was to be served that day.'

He squeezed Venetia's hand. 'I would have telephoned to explain where I was going but I knew you were on one of your shopping expeditions and Elspeth was busy with her committees. I assumed that the meal wouldn't take long, then Bradshaw and I would have a preliminary discussion about his proposition, so I'd be back in my office before the end of the afternoon and home at the usual time.'

'But that wasn't how the afternoon progressed,' said de Silva.

'No, it wasn't. We'd finished lunch. Bradshaw and I were sitting on the verandah with our brandy and cigars when he suddenly turned very pale and clutched his stomach. When I asked him what the matter was, he tried to laugh it off, but it was soon clear that there was something seriously wrong. His face was slick with sweat, and he was having difficulty speaking. When he tried to stand up, he collapsed on the floor.

'I knelt beside him and tried to revive him, but his eyes were completely blank. The servant who'd been attending us had hurried off to fetch Helena. She seemed very flustered, as one might expect, but when I tried to take charge, her manner changed. She said this wasn't the first time her husband had been suddenly taken ill, and she was used to dealing with it. She would call for their doctor to come, and although it was kind of me to offer to help, it wasn't necessary. She and the servants would cope.'

William paused and coughed, the sound rasping in his chest. Venetia gave him an anxious glance. 'Darling, perhaps you've talked for long enough.'

He squeezed her hand. 'The Inspector needs me to finish the story now, my love. Isn't that right, Inspector?'

'It would be very helpful, sir.'

'In the politest possible way then, Helena had made it clear she regarded me as more of a hindrance than a help, so I took my leave. My secretary, Geraldine Fraser, is her niece, so I decided that the best thing to do would be to mention Bradshaw's illness to her. I assumed her aunt would welcome her help, even though she hadn't wanted mine. But I never got that far. A couple of miles short of home, I began to feel unwell myself. I was forced to stop the car and get out when the urge to vomit became overwhelming. After that, I don't know how I managed to drive the rest of the way. I was struggling to breathe, and there was a burning pain on my tongue as if a red-hot poker had been drawn across it. My feet and hands started to tingle, and the feeling became increasingly painful. When I arrived home and tried to get out of the car, I could barely walk. I remember two of the servants helping me inside, but after that everything is a blur. I only vaguely recall Hebden arriving and giving me a shot of something he tells me was morphine. I went out like a light. After that nothing, until I came round earlier today.'

There was a knock at the door and David Hebden came in.

'Ah,' said William, 'the man himself. I've been telling the Inspector about my symptoms, Hebden. Can I leave you to fill in the technicalities?'

'Certainly. As you know, de Silva, Doctor Bradley-Clarke diagnosed a heart attack.'

'But you suspected he was wrong,' said William.

'Yes, not that I'd take too critical a view of his opinion, since the tests that were sent to the laboratory came back negative, and in most cases, that would be relied on as conclusive. If you'd been able to describe your symptoms at the time, it would have been a different matter, but of course that wasn't on the cards.'

He turned to de Silva. 'Anyway, now that we're in possession of more facts, with the assistance of my botanist friend who's something of a specialist in poisons, Bradley-Clarke has come around to the view that William was poisoned. His description of his symptoms indicates that the poison employed may have been aconitine, a substance derived from the common plant monkshood. Its other names are Wolfsbane or Devil's Helmet, due to the shape of its flowers. It's bitter tasting and highly toxic. Even a small amount can kill. Until the beginning of this century, it was sometimes employed in medicine to lower the heartbeat or treat localised inflammation, but the margin of error was so narrow that it ceased to be used. It's hard to detect too, meaning that it's particularly attractive to anyone who wants to use it for a nefarious purpose.'

De Silva noticed that Venetia had turned pale.

'Apart from the burning and tingling sensations William described to me earlier,' Hebden went on, 'the medical term for which is paraesthesia, symptoms include difficulty in breathing, unconsciousness, and ventricular fibrillation, commonly referred to as heart attack. Without wishing to bore you, the movement of sodium ions in heart cells triggers a contraction. A coordinating contraction caused by the release of potassium results in a heartbeat. After each heartbeat, the cells must reset, and the sodium and potassium return to their original positions to allow the process to be repeated. When aconitine enters the body, it binds preferentially to a site on the sodium ion channel and activates it, but instead of the corresponding contraction taking place, the channel stays open, and therefore the cells cannot reset. My botanist friend likens it to trying to empty a bath with the taps still running. Aconitine is very potent. He believes William only ingested a minute amount, or he wouldn't have survived.'

'What about Mr Bradshaw?' asked de Silva. 'You said he was taken ill.'

'He wasn't one of my patients,' said Hebden. 'But I recalled that a colleague of mine lost a patient on the same day, and we had to postpone a meeting we'd arranged. Of course, there might have been no connection, but the timing was thought-provoking, so I telephoned my colleague. He confirmed that the patient was Bradshaw, and he had certi-fied the cause of his death as a heart attack.'

'Do you remember what you ate at the Bradshaws', sir?' asked de Silva.

'Apart from the beef of which Bradshaw was so proud? The usual accompaniments, roast potatoes, carrots, Yorkshire pudding, and of course horseradish sauce. We followed with treacle tart.'

'Did anything taste strange?'

William shrugged. 'It was all as one would expect. In fact, the meal was excellent.'

'Did the whole party eat everything that was served?'

'No, as I've told Hebden, Helena Bradshaw passed on the horseradish.' He frowned. 'There was a bit of unpleasantness over that. There wasn't any on the table and Bradshaw kicked up a fuss. Helena said she'd forgotten to tell the cook to order some, but he wasn't having any of it. He insisted on a thorough search of the kitchen. Said a true Englishman couldn't eat roast beef without horseradish sauce. Personally, I wasn't fussed. I'm not particularly fond of the stuff, too peppery for my taste. When a dish of it arrived after all, I only took a dab of it to be polite. I noticed Bradshaw told the servant who was waiting on him to pile it onto his plate.'

De Silva turned to Hebden. 'Could this aconitine have been hidden in the sauce?'

'The pepperiness would be likely to disguise its bitter taste. According to my botanist friend, aconitine is hard to extract from the plant. In order to give it in pill or liquid form, the process would need to be conducted in laboratory conditions. Where it's administered by someone without access to those, it can be given by using the root in its natural state, either grated or chopped then mixed with something strong tasting. The root resembles that of horseradish.'

'So, gentlemen,' said MacDonald, 'I think we've found the answer, don't you? And by disliking the sauce, I avoided Bradshaw's fate.'

'The question is,' said Hebden, 'who prepared the sauce? Wouldn't you say it's time we paid a visit to Helena Bradshaw, de Silva?'

'Yes, I would.'

* * *

'Do you think Helena Bradshaw is aware of the properties of monkshood?' asked Hebden as de Silva drove them to the Bradshaws' house. He had already commiserated over the damage to the Morris.

'I'm willing to bet that she is. I remember coming across her at the autumn flower show and she seemed to be a keen and knowledgeable gardener. Monkshood is a dangerous plant not normally used as an ornamental. If we can establish that she grows it in her garden, it would indicate that she wanted to use it to poison her husband. And it's not hard to find a motive, I'm told he was a brute of a man, and I saw evidence of it myself at the show.'

'My colleague said Bradshaw had a history of heart problems, so he had no reason to be suspicious about the cause of death, but Bradshaw's sudden demise also fits with what we know about aconitine.'

'This business William MacDonald mentioned with the horseradish sauce,' said de Silva. 'It may be true that Helena dislikes it, but her prime reason for not taking any may well have been that she knew it was potentially lethal. If so, she must have been thoroughly alarmed when Bradshaw brought an unexpected guest home to lunch. I wonder whether Geraldine Fraser took part in any plot to dispose of Bradshaw. Did you know that she was Helena Bradshaw's niece?'

'Not until William mentioned it.'

De Silva slowed the Morris as they rounded a series of tight bends then speeded up again when the road straightened. 'She may have been the lady who called the hospital to ask after William's progress and didn't leave her name, but I'm not sure how much to read into that.'

Before long they reached the Bradshaws' residence. Only two of the ground-floor windows were lit, and there was no sign of activity, but de Silva made out several cars on the drive, including a black Bentley. He thought he had seen it before then remembered the funeral party in the churchyard and the two ladies veiled in black. They might well have been Helena and Geraldine, and the occasion Cyril Bradshaw's funeral.

'Are you planning to speak to Helena before doing anything else?' asked Hebden.

'Yes, I think it's best, even though we aren't in possession of as much evidence as I'd like to have, I don't want to risk her getting away.'

Hebden looked uncomfortable. 'Dashed awkward questioning a lady about her husband's death.'

'I'm afraid police work often is.'

The door took so long to be answered that they began to wonder if the house was deserted, but at last it opened. The servant who stood there peered anxiously into the darkness, his demeanour not helped when he saw De Silva's uniform.

'Is the memsahib in?' asked de Silva.

'No, sahib, has something happened to her?'

De Silva ignored the question. 'What about her niece?'

'She's here some of the time, sahib, but not now. Both the ladies have gone away.'

De Silva's heart sank. It sounded as though Geraldine had been aware of a plot to kill Bradshaw. Perhaps even part of it. If only he had been able to speak to William sooner. 'Did they say when they would be coming back?'

'No, sahib.'

'And where have they gone?'

'Forgive me, sahib,' the man said, looking more anxious than ever, 'I do not know.'

'There must be someone else we can speak to who does,' said Hebden impatiently. 'We'd better come in.'

'I will fetch Chandrasin.'

Whilst they waited, de Silva surveyed the gloomy hall with its treacle-coloured wooden floor, ugly furniture, and oil paintings of gory hunting spoils. With her love of gardens and flowers, he doubted the décor had been Helena Bradshaw's choice.

The grizzled-haired man who shortly arrived had a much more confident air about him than the first servant. 'What's this all about, Inspector?' he asked. 'It's very late.'

'We're looking for Memsahib Bradshaw and her niece. Your man says they've gone away without saying where they were going.'

'That's correct,' said Chandrasin carefully.

'Was anyone else with them?'

'No.'

'We'd like to see the kitchens and speak with your cook,' said Hebden.

A flicker of surprise crossed Chandrasin's face, but he beckoned them to follow him. They left the gloomy hall behind and went through a green baize door, arriving at a flight of broad, shallow stone steps that led down to a large kitchen. A breath of air came from barred windows set in deep embrasures. There was an enormous blackened range, with hooks on either side from which hung pots and pans, and a row of butler's sinks where two cook boys were busy scraping from various bowls what was likely to have been the remnants of the servants' supper. There were also numerous doors, presumably leading to storerooms and pantries. A man with a hawkish nose and black hair fastened in a tight bun on the top of his head sat at a massive table with a wooden top that had been scrubbed to a stone-like smoothness. A glass containing arrack stood at his elbow.

'This is Erajh, our cook. Erajh, the Inspector and his companion have some questions for you.'

A thin wisp of smoke drifted from Erajh's lips as he stubbed out the beedi he had been smoking and got to his feet. 'What would you like to know, sahibs?'

'I understand that you served roast beef on the day that Sahib Bradshaw was taken ill,' said de Silva.

'The beef was good quality and thoroughly cooked. The way Sahib Bradshaw liked it.'

'We're not questioning that, but there was a problem about the horseradish sauce to go with it, wasn't there?'

Erajh shrugged. 'I know it was ordered and delivered but, on the day, we couldn't find it.' He looked sour. 'Sahib Bradshaw was angry. He must have it. Eventually, we found it.' He pointed to a cream-painted Welsh dresser that displayed a rosebud-printed porcelain tea set. 'In one of the teapots. Some silly prank.' He glared at the two cook boys.

'Were any of you responsible?' asked de Silva sternly.

They both shook their heads.

'Apart from you and your staff, did any of the family come to the kitchen before lunch was served?'

Erajh thought for a moment. 'Memsahib Bradshaw came. She wanted to be sure the beef was well cooked. There must be no blood showing.'

'Did she go anywhere near the dresser?'

Erajh shrugged. 'I'm not sure. We were very busy making the final preparations.'

De Silva thanked him, and he, Hebden, and Chandrasin went back to the family's part of the house. 'We'd like to see the garden now,' said de Silva.

'But it is dark, sahib.'

'No matter, I have a torch in my car, but an oil lamp would also be useful.'

Chandrasin went to fetch a lamp. 'Shall I come with you, sahibs?' he asked when he came back.

'There's no need, just give us a brief idea of how the garden is laid out.'

At the back of the house there was a broad, stone-paved terrace with steps that led down to a lawn. Even with the oil lamp as well as de Silva's torch, it wasn't easy to see very far ahead.

'I hope we don't have to investigate that wilderness area

Chandrasin mentioned,' said Hebden. 'Shall we try the kitchen garden first?'

A wrought-iron gate in a high brick wall led to the garden where fruit and vegetables were grown for the house. De Silva felt some pangs of envy as they searched long beds neatly planted with rows of vegetables. Espaliered fruit trees stood in regimented rows and there were swathes of flowers for cutting whose fragrance perfumed the warm night air. This must be Helena's doing, thought de Silva.

At the far end of the garden, they found greenhouses and potting sheds built against the garden's surrounding brick wall. Hebden took the oil lamp and went into the first potting shed, leaving de Silva to explore the greenhouses. He had finished with the first one he came to when he heard Hebden call out. He went to join him.

'Have you found something?'

'I think I may have done.' He pointed to a bench where there was a small knife on a wooden board. Picking it up, he ran his thumb along the side of the blade. 'Well sharpened,' he observed. 'And look at this.'

De Silva shone his torch on the bench and saw a blackened kettle, and a small gas ring with a pan beside it. There was also a caddy decorated with a picture of Queen Victoria and a chipped brown china mug. De Silva lifted the lid of the caddy and smelled the spicy aroma of tea.

'It might just be that someone likes to make themselves a hot drink,' said Hebden, 'but one doesn't need a knife for that, and if there's a kettle, what is the pan for?'

De Silva looked around. 'If someone used the knife to chop monkshood, they would surely take the precaution of wearing gloves.'

'There's a pair.' Hebden reached to the back of the bench and picked up some gloves made of a coarse dun-coloured cloth. 'Here you are.' He held one up for de Silva to see. 'From the size, they belong to a woman. Still no plant

179

though. Perhaps we'll have to explore that wilderness after all.'

Back in the open air, de Silva noticed that beyond the last of the greenhouses, there was a large heap of compost with several wheelbarrows upended against it. It was worth a try before tackling the rest of the garden.

'Where are you going now?' asked Hebden. 'I hope you're not suggesting there's something buried in that heap. The stink's bad enough at this distance.'

'Not under it, but behind it. It would be a good place to hide the plant where it would also flourish.'

The pungent smell of rotting dung and vegetation filled de Silva's nostrils as he wheeled one of the barrows out of the way and edged behind the heap, feeling the ground become spongy under his feet. Directing the beam of his torch into the space, he saw something glimmer. It was a tall plant with spires of blue flowers, each one shaped like a tiny helmet, the shape that gave the plant its old name: the Devil's Helmet. Perhaps because he knew of its dangers, he felt a sinister power emanate from it. 'I think we've found what we're looking for.'

CHAPTER 15

It was nearly midnight by the time de Silva arrived home, but Jane was still up and met him in the hall.

'I'm so glad you're back, I was beginning to worry. Emerald telephoned earlier and told me she'd heard from Venetia. Some story about roast beef and horseradish sauce, but Venetia was worn out and not explaining it very well. Does it mean you've found the culprit?' Her nose wrinkled. 'Where have you been, dear? What's that terrible smell?'

De Silva looked down at his uniform and realised that there were stains of manure on his trousers. 'Sorry, I'll go and clean up.'

'Have you eaten?'

'Hebden and I had a bit of dahl and rice at a roadside stall. He'd left his car at the hospital, so I took him to collect it, and we stopped on the way.'

'If you're still hungry, I'll ask cook to prepare something for you.'

'Don't disturb him. At this time of night, I'm happy to make do with a glass of water.'

* * *

'So as we thought, Elspeth and Douglas simply took advantage of William being poisoned,' said Jane when a short time afterwards, water in hand, de Silva had explained what had been happening. 'And no doubt Helena Bradshaw didn't intend the horseradish to be eaten by anyone except her husband. Poor lady, she must have been desperate to do such a thing. Do the MacDonalds know everything now?'

'No, but of course we ought to tell them soon. I'll telephone the hospital first thing in the morning and speak to Venetia. She'll be very upset by the news. She liked Geraldine and most likely she met Helena too. We can only speculate as to how early on Geraldine was involved in Helena's plan to kill Cyril Bradshaw. She may not have confided in Geraldine and asked for her help until she feared the truth would come out.'

'Do you think there's a chance of catching up with them?'

'It's too late to do anything tonight, but in the morning, I'll get Prasanna and Nadar onto alerting as many police stations as possible. They can ask at the railway station too in case they got away by train, although I think they would be more likely to use a car. I know Geraldine has one and I don't recall seeing it at the Bradshaw house.'

'Do you think they'll try to leave the country?'

'I expect so, and Colombo would be the nearest point of departure. I'll telephone police headquarters down there as well and speak to my old friend Rudi Chockalingham. I'm sure he'll be prepared to help.'

* * *

'We'll do our best,' said Rudi when de Silva telephoned the following morning and told him about the case, 'but I must warn you not to expect miracles. We're very busy down here with the celebrations coming to a head.'

'Yes, you must be.'

Rudi sighed. 'It's a great moment in our island's history,

but I confess, I'll be glad when all the pomp and pageantry is behind us. This Duke of Gloucester and the bigwigs he brings with him have no idea of the headaches they're causing me, and even if they did know, I doubt they would care much. But for us, it is a matter of honour that everything should go like clockwork.'

'And I'm sure it will,' said de Silva.

'How are you doing in Nuala?'

'I must admit, I've not had much time recently to pay attention to the arrangements for the big day.'

'That's understandable. Well, I must be getting on. If there's anything to report, I'll be in touch.'

De Silva thanked him and put the receiver back in its cradle.

'How was Rudi?' asked Jane when he returned to the drawing room.

'Busy with final preparations for the big day, but he says he'll do his best to help. After I've been to the station to give Prasanna and Nadar their orders, I'd better go up to the Residence and tell Archie how things stand.'

* * *

'So, Bill MacDonald was unlucky enough to be in the wrong place at the wrong time, poor fellow,' said Archie when de Silva brought him up to date. 'Of course Elspeth and Douglas will still stand trial for kidnapping Venetia, but the conduct of that will be under your new regime.'

His eyes drifted to a photograph on his desk. It showed him in fishing gear with his old dog Darcy by his side. 'A lot of changes in prospect, eh, de Silva? I didn't foresee them when Florence and I came to the island thirty years ago, but the world is a different place since the war.' He cleared his throat. 'Back to your case. I still haven't congratulated you on solving it in the nick of time.'

'I'm afraid there's still work to be done, sir. We're a long way off catching Helena Bradshaw and her niece.'

'Well, do your best, and muster all the help you can. By the way, how's your sergeant getting on?'

'He should be back at work in a couple of days.'

'Good. Any progress on finding out what Tranter was up to?'

'No yet, he's still refusing to talk.'

Archie rubbed his chin between his thumb and fore-finger. 'Strange business. You'd better persevere and get to the bottom of it. I can't say I got to know the fellow well, but he didn't seem the violent type. If anything, a bit of a ladies' man.'

As he left the Residence, de Silva wondered gloomily what would come first: a solution to the two cases, or Archie's retirement. He would prefer to embark on tackling a new boss and regime with a clean slate.

CHAPTER 16

The news that two ladies answering to the descriptions of Helena and Geraldine had boarded a ship leaving Colombo for India dimmed de Silva's hopes of finding them, but he had better luck with Tranter.

'You look cheerful, dear,' said Jane when he returned home one evening and found her in the drawing room.

'I should do. At last I've got to the bottom of what Laurence Tranter was up to. I think it was the prospect of a conviction for assaulting two police officers that made him decide to talk. It turns out that in between painting portraits and charming the British ladies, he got sucked into an illegal gambling ring in Hatton. At first, he won quite a lot of money but then he started losing heavily. He managed to persuade the boss behind the ring to accept an IOU by claiming that he was about to receive a substantial payment for his portrait commissions, but the man soon became suspicious that he was being lied to. He threatened Tranter who decided to go into hiding. He planned to take the train down to Kandy and on to Colombo once he was satisfied none of the gang were watching for him at the railway station.'

He walked to the sideboard to pour himself a whisky and soda. 'A sherry for you?' he asked Jane.

'Yes please, especially as we have something to celebrate.'

He brought their drinks over and sat down before

continuing his story. 'When I saw Tranter leave the house that day, he was going to find some food. Whilst he was out, he feared that he had been spotted so he didn't want to return immediately in case he was followed. He persuaded an acquaintance to let him spend the rest of the day at their home before he went back to the house.'

He took a sip of whisky. 'When Prasanna turned up, Tranter thought the gambling boss's henchmen had found him after all. In the heat of the moment, he went on the attack and tried to escape.'

'What will happen to him now?'

'He's at Hatton where Inspector Singh has him locked up in the cells. Singh wanted to question him about the gambling ring. It's one Singh's been after for some time. I understand that Tranter's now eager to help the police, hoping no doubt that his cooperation will be taken into account when he's sentenced for assault. It was probably a blessing in disguise for him that we arrested him when we did. He doesn't seem to have much of a talent for making himself inconspicuous. I think his luck with avoiding his pursuers might soon have run out with serious consequences.'

* * *

After dinner they sat on the verandah enjoying the cool of the evening. A light breeze stirred the trees, and the air hummed with the throb of cicadas. There was a faint smell of rain. He would be glad of it for the garden's sake, thought de Silva, but he hoped it wouldn't go on for too long, and especially that it wouldn't mar the independence celebrations.

Stifling a yawn, he shifted in his chair. 'Only a few days to go until the big event. At least Tranter is off my hands, even though there's still no word from India about Helena and Geraldine.'

'Were you really expecting there to be?'

'I suppose not. It's easy to disappear in such a vast country and I dare say the Indian police have enough problems of their own to deal with.'

He stroked Bella's sleek head, and she looked up and gave him a little miaow, showing neat rows of needle-sharp white teeth. From his position under Jane's chair, Billy rolled over lazily and glanced in their direction then curled up and went back to sleep. 'At least someone is relaxed about the state of the world,' said de Silva with a smile. 'I think that in my next life, I might like to come back as a cat.'

'There's a new regime to deal with before then. I wonder if life will really be very different after the handover.'

'I'm sure it will in some respects, not least having to answer to PJ Fernando, this new Commissioner of Police.'

'Do you know anything more about him yet?'

'No, still only that he's currently with the force in Colombo, and arrived after my time. Oh, but I had a word with Rudi Chockalingham today. He says Fernando's very ambitious.'

'Are you suggesting that's a bad thing?'

'Not in general, but I'm not sure how well it will work for Nuala. But then maybe we won't see very much of him. He'll be in charge of several towns in the hill country, not only this one.'

'I saw Florence this afternoon. She looked very tired, poor thing. I felt quite sorry for her. I know she has plenty of servants to help her, but there is a lot to do. She and Archie have lived for so many years at the Residence, and they won't have long to move out. She says she already has dozens of crates stacked up to be taken by the removal men and that's only a start. Their new house is a worry too. You know how particular Florence is. She says that everything in it will need to be replaced.'

De Silva smiled and thought of Archie. At their recent meetings, his boss had often looked rather frayed. De Silva doubted he cared about interior decorating. He had, however, mentioned with evident pleasure that the new bungalow was close to a fishing lake, and the golf course was also nearby.

'I'm glad they've decided to stay on,' said Jane. 'Nuala wouldn't be the same without them.'

CHAPTER 17

Independence Day dawned bright and clear. Still in his dressing gown, de Silva went out to the garden to enjoy a few moments of peace. They would be the last he had for the rest of the day. Early rays of sun sliced through the trees, touching their leaves with gold. Billy and Bella ambled by his side; he bent down to stroke them. 'You've no idea what all the fuss is about, have you? And you won't notice any difference after today.'

He straightened up and contemplated the years ahead. Even on the brink of independence it wasn't easy to visualise how life would change. After the celebrations and the rousing speeches, the real work would begin.

But first, he needed to direct all his attention to Nuala's celebrations. They had been upmost in everyone's mind, often his included, even eclipsing the search for Helena and Geraldine. His hopes of finding them were increasingly slim, and at his most recent meeting with Archie, he'd felt that his boss's were too. Archie soon closed the subject and bent his head over the map laid out on his desk. 'Now, let's get back to the route that our visitors will be taking through town to the Residence,' he'd said. 'Are you sure nothing's been overlooked?'

De Silva had felt a pleasant lightness of heart as he reeled off the arrangements for the umpteenth time.

* * *

'Ah, there you are.' Jane stood at the top of the steps to the verandah. 'Are you ready for breakfast?'

'Certainly.' He twitched the lapel of his dressing gown. 'I'll come as I am and get ready afterwards.'

'Very wise. Delisha has taken so much trouble pressing your dress uniform and polishing the buttons and belt.'

'I might even be able to do the belt up an extra notch,' he said as he ate his eggs. 'With all the rushing around, I think I've lost some weight.'

Jane laughed. 'I'm convinced Archie and Florence have. We British love our ceremonial occasions and a lot of work has to go into making them look effortless. Florence says that with so much responsibility on their shoulders, they've not had a moment to themselves.'

'Hmm, they're not the only ones who've been busy.'

Jane leaned over and patted his hand. 'Of course not, but you know how Florence is.'

An hour later, resplendent in his dress uniform and with the newly repaired Morris polished to within an inch of its life by Jayasena, de Silva set off for the police station.

For several days, whole families had been walking into town from the surrounding villages. Barriers were already set up along the route to the Residence that the British dignitaries and Nuala's new councillors were to take; the civilians drafted in as special constables and the detachment of British soldiers organised by Archie had been tasked with keeping the crowds behind them. All other parts of town were, however, full to bursting. Swarms of excited children darted between the rickshaws, carts, and motor cars on the streets. The air rang with laughter and the babble of conversation. Everyone wore their best clothes, and many had garlands of flowers around their necks. Buildings displayed the new flag, and strings of bunting had turned the façade of the Crown Hotel into a riot of red and gold.

The official procession was due to set off from town at ten o'clock, reaching the Residence at midday. De Silva spent the hours beforehand making sure that those tasked with clearing the route did their job. At last, it was time. The brass band struck up a march and moved forward, the bandsmen's scarlet uniforms flashing like the plumage of exotic birds. A detachment of guards, also in scarlet with black busbies on their heads fell into step behind them with another detachment bringing up the rear behind the official cars. As they passed him, de Silva glimpsed the solemn profiles, black robes, chains of office, pristine white uniforms embellished with gold braid and scarlet epaulettes, elegant frocks, and chic hats of the occupants.

Then the procession faded from sight. As if a dam had burst, the barriers gave way, and the crowds poured out; soon the road disappeared beneath them. For the next few hours there was much eating and drinking then the time came for the town's own procession, with elephants caparisoned in red and gold leading it. Acrobats and dancers followed, dressed in rainbow colours with bells flashing on their anklets and trimming the veils that hid the faces of the women leaving only their eyes on show. Drums and pipes provided a joyous accompaniment. As darkness fell, flares were lit, and the sky fizzed and popped with fireworks.

The party lasted long into the night, with no trouble from the happy crowds. De Silva told Prasanna and Nadar they could join their families and allowed himself to relax a little and enjoy the fun too. He caught sight of Jane and the Hebdens who had been invited to the earlier reception at the Residence and went to join them.

'How did things go at the Residence?' he asked.

Jane gestured to the crowds. 'Very well, although extremely staid in comparison with here.'

'But it was moving when the new flag was raised, wasn't it,' said Emerald.

'Yes. Archie handed over his seals of office and the proclamation of independence was read out.'

'I'm sorry I wasn't there to hear it,' said de Silva.

Emerald kissed his cheek, and Hebden shook his hand. 'All the same, congratulations, old chap.'

Jane linked her arm in his. 'Isn't it all just so wonderful, dear.'

De Silva contemplated the momentous sensation of having his country back. He wasn't sure *wonderful* was a strong enough word for the changes and no doubt the challenges that lay ahead.

Above them, another firework exploded in the sky into myriad stars and the crowds whooped and cheered.

'Yes,' he said, cupping his hand over Jane's, 'it is indeed, wonderful.'

Printed in Dunstable, United Kingdom